T0367832

# GHOSTS

By Jean Marie Rusin

Edited by K.D.

authorHOUSE®

AuthorHouse™
1663 Liberty Drive
Bloomington, IN 47403
www.authorhouse.com
Phone: 1-800-839-8640

Published by AuthorHouse 6/7/2013

ISBN: 978-1-4817-6366-0 (sc)
ISBN: 978-1-4817-6365-3 (e)

Any people depicted in stock imagery provided
by Thinkstock are models, and such images are
being used for illustrative purposes only.
Certain stock imagery © Thinkstock.

This book is printed on acid-free paper.

Because of the dynamic nature of the Internet, any
web addresses or links contained in this book may have
changed since publication and may no longer be valid.

The views expressed in this work are solely those of the author
and do not necessarily reflect the views of the publisher, and
the publisher hereby disclaims any responsibility for them.

# TABLE OF CONTENTS

# ONE STORMY NIGHT

It was the night of séance when everything happened that night, when the murder occurs and the window shatter and peoples screaming that night and no one in sight and then the lights when out, and then it was dead silent.

The winds blow in and then they saw that shadowy figure standing in front of them why did you conjure this sprit into this house, you said that you loss a son and I bought him back he is not mine.

Then he came closer to us and we were in a trance and then the lights when out and it happened, everyone was silent and not a sound heard.

What have you done? I have not, if came from the walls of this house, you are lying why should lies, we are danger here and we need to leave immediately and don't understand what I am saying to you? Yes but I didn't want to be here for the séance but you force me to comes and now I don't know if we will be unable to escape this nightmare.

Why I would like to know, because you have betrayed me and but my friends didn't why are you putting them in danger, well this the revenge that I had planned for month and now, you will paid with your life and your friends too.

I am begged you to let us go and I will not tell soul, no you won't because I will killed you all you are evil man and I didn't betrayed you, your mind is confuse with lies been told, now it is time that you paid what you took from me, no I have taken but you stole from me and you need to stop lying to my face.

1

Let them go and you can killed, no they will watched and one by one you will be all dead. Then Joe said don't do it, I am begging for my life, Jon would listen, and the first shot was firing and Joe fell to the ground said, why? Then more shots were firing and in the library and they lay dead and Joe tried to escape, but somehow he trip and the gun fired and all five bodies lay in the library on the night of " Friday 13th and the police arrives and yellow tape wrap around the ground and police tried to found out what happened?

They looked around and took some evidence and said we have unsolved murders that occur here and something went wrong. Yes they were having a séance and no explained here, I know and they took out five bodies in body bags and we have to find out what happened here?

But we will take the evidence to the lab and hope it will tell us.

So far seem like no intruder in the house, yes and what else?

Seems like someone was inside when the murder occurs, well it was not a force entry the killer was inside, well where is killer? That is a good question, but before left one of the police officer saw shadow from the window.

Did you see that? No, your eyes are tricking you, looks I don't sees anything.

They drove away from the house and they felt the chill and the wind and then they drove away and it was gone. Meanwhile faces were staring and saying we are stuck here forever here, what are saying, we are dead, what, he killed us, who did, the man standing next too you, yes it Marko, why did you killed us?

Well you friend of Joe and you came to this séance and I just killed you all, we didn't do anything to you and you killed us, so the house didn't let you go and you ended up dead too!

I guess it backfire and I am here too for a reason, yes to reminder us what you have done to us and keep us from going to the light.

2

Then all the doors and windows shut and ghosts were walking in the house and it happened 10 year ago and still ghosts wander the night, one night all the doors and windows open and then shut. The house was empty and ghost's walks the halls and library of the house, and it occurs every Friday 13th and it repeat the murder each times.

Marko said to the peoples that he killed, I cannot be dead, and the other four person said, you are and Marko said, been curse to be in this house and I need to leave, no the house is keeping us for a reason.

Time when by and Marko, Jon and Joe said, we are dead and when I tried to step out but I am unable to do so!

Then Joe said why did you kill us? Well you were in my ways and I just killed you all because you were here no reason you are crazy.

No, I have been pushed around by Joe and I need to teach he a lesson and you murder us all, you are insane. No I am not!

Marko left the library and left the four and wander into the other room and looked into the kitchen and tried to open the door and but it stayed close.

The four stayed in the library and Joe said I don't know when it happened but we are here long time, how do you know. Looks at us, do we look different.

# 10 YEAR AFTER THE MURDERS

 New owner moving in and they had a teenager son and he was a loner and had trouble in school and they decided to live in the country and move out of the city, the night they move in their son Josh, Josh when inside the house and he went to the bedroom near the library and his mom and dad said I thought it were be our bedroom and Josh said I really like this room and they said okay.

Karen and Jeff said we will be in the kitchen and so if you are hungry come to the kitchen and I will make diner for us, fine mom said Josh.

Josh went to his bedroom and shut the door and about one minute later he heard a knock at his door and he said mom leave me alone.

Then he open the door and no one was there and then he close the door and put on his headset and listen to his music and about half hour later his mom came in and said I been calling you and you didn't answer.

Josh got up and said I will be right there and then Leo suddenly stops and said mom did you felt that's? No, what are you saying, I feel someone is watching us, don't let your dad here you saying that. Okay I won't!

Come on Josh I don't want your dad to be furious, but don't says anything to him, I won't but I don't like this place.

It is creeping, no it is not but it is out in the country and I don't like living in the woods, and Josh left his room and then the black flies were buzzing.

About one hour later Josh got up from the table and when into his room and Karen and Jeff said what wrong with him, he just need a adjust of the move and he will be fine.

Are you should he is having those the illusion again? Tell me the truth Karen yes he is, so he needs to get some help and I don't want to move again!

Josh will be fine, you know that he hate change and so he will adjust, soon has he started school and make friends, hope that your right, I believe I am.

Later that night Josh heard his parents speaking about him and he was not too happy about it so he came up to his parents and said this house is haunted.

Jeff looked at his son and said I am going to gets you some help, but I am not making up things are happening here, I don't want to hears your nonsense so we will to DR. Bob, and he will describe some medication, you think that I am having episodes again but I am not, stayed in my room and you will sees what I sees, stop it Josh.

Josh stood up and left his mom and dad at the table and Karen follow him and said I cannot believe that you are seeing things again!

Then Josh said leave me alone and he slams the door behind and Karen said you cannot act this way, keep the door open, and Josh got up and said fine!

Later that night Josh was up and looking up at the ceiling and he saw a black shadowy figure walking toward him and he screamed and yelled and then Jeff came into the room and said, I have called Dr. Bob and he will drop by later too sees you I don't need a shrink dad but we need a paranormal too comes because we have "GHOSTS", stop it Josh you are scaring your mom, well I did see a dark shadow, and it came close to me. So we need to put him on valium and overnight at the hospital and Josh said I am not going and you cannot force me, yes you are going? Mom why don't you believe me, I am telling the truth and you are in danger, stop this Josh, go to the car and Karen said don't listen what your son is saying, you are crazy just like your son and Jeff storm out of the house and Josh said we need to get out of the house now…

But Karen said no, but my mom you don't believe me? How can I believe you when you told his lies in the past and we had to move here?

Mom I never lies and I was seeing things and they were after me, who were after you, Shadow Peoples" that is nonsense, and you must been high on a drug, then Josh went up to his room and shut the door and lock it.

About one hour later, Jeff came home and said where he is? I am going to take him and he will get the help that he need.

No, I am not putting him into the hospital, later that night Josh open his door and he thought that he heard someone calling his name and Josh answer and said what do you wants from me? Then he when into his room lie down on the bed and felt a chill and cold breathe and now Josh knew that he was not alone.

Meanwhile Jeff and Karen were discussion about what they were going to do with Josh, and about half hour later, Josh had a bruise on his arm.

What happened to him? I don't know. Tells us the truth, why do you harm yourself? I don't they did too me, who are they? GHOSTS.

Jeff grab Josh and took him in the car, Karen said don't take him tonight!

#  VOICES

Josh got away and when into his bedroom and lay on the bed and then he saw those black flies coming toward him and started to bite him on the face and then Josh fell on the floor and he saw the figure that was about to bite his hand and then he ran out of his room and fell from flight of stair and Karen tried to wake him but then they called the ambulance and he was still out of cold and they couldn't wake him up, and they did CPR on Josh, and he was seeing so many faces, and voices and they are here and they will not leave me alone, they wanted me, who wants you? The ghosts in this house and they will not let me go, Josh do you hears us. Josh, mom and dad I don't know where you are, Karen said you are scaring me, Josh, I don't sees mom and dad.

Josh was hearing the voices louder and louder and that he had to block his ears and he couldn't take it and wanted to leave his room but they were not let him and then Karen came up to Josh what going on with you? But Josh were not answer her, and then she called Jeff, something scare him and he is not speaking to me, because it is mental state, no I believe it something more going on and you believe that he is seeing GHOSTS, yes I think he is. I think that Josh is not crazy , he were not make up the story, because he wants attention, probably telling the truth, I think you both need helped, Jeff said I cannot take this and Jeff walks out the house and Karen said why do you always runaway when there is a problem, no I don't but you never to listen and discuss, I need time alone fine, Jeff get into his car and drive away and then Josh said we cannot stayed here, voice said it will killed us, stop Josh, I don't want to hear that Josh, so Josh when back to his room and then Karen decided to take a shower, and Karen said to Josh I am going to take a shower and he said okay mom, Josh was sitting in his room, the voices were getting louder and louder, and Josh put a pillow over his head and meanwhile his mom was taking the shower and then she was about to step out, and it grab her and wrap her around, and now she was yelling for help but Josh didn't hears her.

About half hour later, Jeff came home and heard her screaming and he ran upstairs and the door were not open and then he felt a chill and then the door open and Karen was laying on the floor and Karen said I am glad to sees you and he asked what happened but Karen was not sure what to says and kept to herself, and Jeff came close to Karen and Karen was very quiet and said nothing that night. Meanwhile, Josh fell asleep and about 2 am Josh woke up and he was lying on the floor and he thought to himself what happen and then it grab him and bite his arm, and then Josh receive a few bruises on the arm and the next morning he acting normally and didn't mention what happened. But the voices were getting worst and Josh had no one to talked about it.

Josh also got a warning to leave the house but he didn't wanted to end up in a mental ward, so things were not getting better but more activities occurs each day and Josh, every day from school, Josh went to his room, Josh was being like hermit, and Karen tried to talked to him but he refuse to listen to his mom.

Josh said leave me alone and then walks into his room and slam the door behind him, and I don't want to talk with you now.

Karen said to Josh I know that something wrong with you is it anxiety? No mom but we do have ghosts in this house. No it is your imagination, no it is not and they warn me that we will die here, stop it. I don't want to hear it.

But the voices got louder and louder that Josh cover his ears and didn't listen to anyone that spoke to him and his parents were furious with Josh and they wanted to send him away but the house kept inside his room and isolate from the rest and now Karen and Jeff were very worry about Josh and Josh didn't even go to school, and the situation was getting worst and not better, so Jeff advice that his Dr. Bob were comes over and check him out.

But Dr. Bob refuse to comes over and he heard about the death in the house and the haunted house, Jeff said to him what wrong why are you refusing to comes to the house, are you paranoid no I am not stepping a foot in that house, tells me why? Don't you know the history of the house about the fires and then they found five bodies, and they were murder and they are saying that the five are still in the house and they are ghosts, and you listen to that nonsense, it is not nonsense and you should leave your house on Friday the 13th and it will happened again, and then Jeff didn't wanted to listen anymore and Karen said is DR. Bob coming over and Jeff said nope we need to take Josh to him, no way, Josh will not go and he locked his doors and we need to get through too him, and meanwhile Josh was hearing voices that warn him to leave and they were all around and Josh couldn't take it and he was about to open the door and it were not tells him so he yelled out and no one heard him.

"Then the phone rang and Jeff answered and no one was there!

Jeff called out to Josh and said did you call? Josh said why were I called and then once again the phone rang and it was silent and it suddenly hung up and then Jeff said, I will called star 69 and sees who calling us.

But the phone suddenly went dead and then the storm came and then the lights, went out and then Josh heard footstep do you hears that dad? Karen said well I don't know what I am hearing I think it the storm doing the sound. Comes on mom I think you know that we are living with ghosts, I don't want to hear this foolish about paranormal, do you understand what I am saying.

Go to your room, Jeff said listen too your mom, fine and Josh when into his room and they were staring at Josh, we are going to get you...

Josh went to his bed and lay down and put cover up and one minute the cover were off him and he felt a chill and cold breathe, from his mouth and he knew that he was not alone and few black flies were buzzing around him and now he felt trapped, Josh got up from his bed and wanted to leave his room, but was unable to do, and Josh didn't panic and he felt that someone touch him and it was like wanted to hurt him, and he pried open the door but it pull him back.

Then he fell to the floor and it lifting him up and spin him twice and then it was gone, and Josh just lay on the floor and was scare, stunned what just happen to him. Josh didn't tell his parents what occurs and he was really afraid and thought this moment that he was losing his mind.

Time when by and three days nothing happened but on the fourth day it happened again and this time he was laying on the bed and it was pulling him and it were not let go, and then it just stops and one voice said you are next! Josh said to his dad that he wanted to visit his grandma, and Jeff said if grandma said it is okay and you will go and Josh said I wants to go tonight, so what going on Josh, you were not believe me if I told you, try me.

About two hour later, Jeff got a called from his mom and she said I will not allow your son in my house and he is evil, and Jeff said what are you saying about my son?

Josh overheard the discuss and Josh walks out of the house and Karen follow him and what are you doing? I am unwanted so I will put up my tent and I sleep in the woods, no you are not. I am not staying in the house, neither.

Talk to and let me understand what you are saying, well I believe this house is haunted and if I stayed I will died, stop, I don't like that crazy talking that you are saying, and you are only 15 year old and you do not have my permission to sleep in the woods, so I guess you will be coming to my funeral?

No, you will be fine and go to your room this moment and I don't want no argument from you don't you understand what going on, don't be this ways!

# ACTIVITY

Karen was sitting in the living room and she was watching the TV and then suddenly the lights were flickering and then the door open and thought it was Jeff that came home, and then Karen looked around and it was silent and then a big banged on the door and then like a hundred of flies were in the room and then they landed on her face. Karen started to scream and no one heard her and then the next morning Josh came down and saw his mom laying on the floor and said what happened I got attacked by black flies and Josh said I told you there are ghosts in our home, and Karen said to Josh somehow flies just came in by screen, comes on my mom, you still don't believe what I am saying too you, and I am leaving the house and I am not coming back, I feel that I am in danger and you and dad and we need to convince him to leave.

About one minute later there was an eerie feeling and heavy feeling in the house and then something push Karen to the floor.

About a minute later, the windows would like they were frosted and Karen felt a cold breathe and now she knew that she was not alone and then Josh decided to pull his mom out the house and but the door were not open and about five minutes later, the doors and windows were closing and opening and somehow Josh got inside and Josh ended up on the ceiling and Karen said, I need to gets you down and then it push her down and Josh said you have to run and don't looks back and I am not leaving you and then it stop for a moment and Josh was pulling upstairs and Karen couldn't save her son from the poltergeist and it was too fight it off and Karen barely escape the house and then Jeff came home and asked what going on? Our son is taken by a ghost, I don't want to hear that story, I don't believe in ghosts! Don't you see your son anywhere? No but he is just playing games with you, no he is not.

Karen said to Jeff we need to find him now, before it is too late, I don't what you are saying and I had a bad day at work, because of big black flies.

Yes we have big black flies in the attic and where Father Frank got attack by those flies, and about a minute later, Karen said don't you hear Josh?

He is playing you and he will be grounded, do you sees him, right now, no I don't sees him, then Jeff said make me dinner and Karen open the fridge and saw the foods spoils and cockroaches on the foods, and I cannot cook you anything, comes here looks at the foods?

Jeff looks and the foods look okay, well if you don't want make dinner for me just tell me. Karen the foods is spoil and those ugly bugs, at this time Karen was hearing echo of Josh, and then the lights flicker and suddenly got dark and Jeff thought that Josh was playing with lights and our five minutes, Jeff felt a chill in the air and then the door rang, Jeff when to answer and no one there. But I do sees a shadow, and once again the doorbell rang and Jeff when to answers the door and there was an old man, and then the phone rang and Jeff when to answer the phone and then came back to the door and the old gray man was gone. Then Jeff went to the kitchen and thought he wanted some steak and he took out of the fridge and then he saw it cockroach and moss and he called out to Karen said what are buying old foods, no I am not.

Then he walks to the counter and something grabs his arms and was not let him go! He called out to Karen helped me; I am coming; now you believe your son and me? Yes I do, and I think that we have five ghosts, you don't say!

Later that night Josh was thinking about coming back to the house but then he thought it about it he camp out but still was touch my the ghost and warns him to leave, but he stayed. At this point Josh when toward to the house and was about to walks inside and someone push him out. But the second attempt Josh got inside and saw his mom on the ceiling and his dad laying on the floor and then somehow he pulled his dad out of the house and then step back into the house and then door shut and he was trapped and his mom fell from the ceiling and crawl to him and said let me out, now, but Josh was like frozen at that time and but Karen drag herself out but at first the door were not open then Karen was out of the house but she was yelling at Josh to come out.

Josh couldn't move, and Karen and Jeff said come out of the house and Josh said go away from here now, we are not leaving you in this house, please I am begged you do not to comes back inside, you comes out now!!! I cannot leave I need to find out what happed in this house, you only 15 year old and you are my child,, and I want you to be with us, sorry mom, they wants me too stayed with them, I will not allowance it. Later that night Josh walks back to his room and then shut the door, and his mom and dad stood outside and said, Jeff I am going to gets Josh, your not going alone, I am going with you, so Jeff tried to open the door but it were not open but meanwhile Josh had a chill in the room and the ghosts standing next to his bed and then he saws the dark shadow walking across his room and try to pull him from the bed.

# FIVE GHOSTS

Josh was looking around his room and suddenly he saw them all standing in his room and the room was next to the library where the murders occurs and Josh was getting scare and didn't know what was going happen next, one old lady sat on his bed and then one was pulling him to the floor and he couldn't believe that the floor just open up and he was about to fall in, but somehow Josh manage to run of his room and his dad grab him and push him downstairs and out of the door, and meanwhile Karen was trapped and they didn't want to let her go, " The Five Ghosts" were in the room. Now Karen was not alone, and those black flies were buzzing, and they were on her face and body. Jeff tried to remove them but they when after him and Josh came in and said, you know what they are? They are the ghosts of those five peoples that were murders ten years ago and now they want us to be with them.

What are you saying they going too tried to kill us? I hope not.

But Josh hesitates about the situation was not getting better and then Jeff said we need to leave tonight, because tomorrow will be Friday the 13th.

You don't says the event will occurs the same time like ten year ago, I don't want to hear that, well you need to be ready to leave tonight I cannot leave because I am stuck in this room and you need to get me out now.

After Friday the 13th we can go back home and the ghosts will

15

not touch us, so you are saying tonight we will be going to the hotel and stayed there.

But how do we gets your mom out of this room and Josh said let me go in and they will let her go, and I am not going to sacrifice you, son. Just take mom and I will be in back of you, you will? Yes I will.

About one hour later Jeff and Karen were safe out of the house and Josh was still inside and Jeff said he was going behind us and now he is not here.

Jeff was about to step in the house and Josh slam the door behind him and said dad I am in back of you so let go now...

Josh, push his dad and mom and then step back into the house and it was locked and Jeff and Karen tried to open the door and it locked.

Karen was screaming and yelling and said Josh you come out this instantly, but Josh was trapped with the five ghosts and he cannot die. But then the door open and Josh step out and then I thought you were a goner, no I just show them to the light, but they didn't go.

"Then Jeff and Karen and Josh saw the five ghosts staring out of the window, but then they saw a one and it looks like a "DEMON".

We cannot stayed here, but Josh said they are not going to chase us away from our home, so what do we do? We called a paranormal investigate and they can get rid of them, and we will get our home back, and Josh will be back to normal. Mom you cannot says that I am not normal but I do sees ghosts and what they wants from me, and I am not scare but I do want to go back inside.

No, you are going back we are leaving this place now, and we are not coming back. But Josh sneaks out of the car and once again he went inside of the house and Karen was looking for Josh where did he go? I don't know I think that Josh is under the spell and I think we better go inside no way I am not going to get killed, I am staying out here, you are such a coward, no I am not. Go and get your son now, fine, but if I do get killed I will go after you, and what, then Jeff step inside and then he went inside and there was no trance of Josh, and Jeff looked in each room and meanwhile Karen was standing in the yard and Josh came up and said where is dad? Karen said he was looking for you, I just took a walks on the ground and now I will get dad from the house and be careful, I know will be midnight, and it will be Friday the 13th, yes I know. So Jeff looked around and he was about to walk out and he saw his son standing at near the stairs and was about to grab him but then didn't wanted to let him go, Josh, don't go, I need to save dad, and Karen said I am going with you no, I don't you all die because they wants me.

Later that night almost midnight and they have about five minutes and time is ticking and Josh almost got his dad and his mom still waiting outside for them to come out and then Josh find his dad and open the door and then Josh was stuck in the house and then Jeff and Karen banged and banged at the door and nothing and meanwhile Jeff was surrounded by the five ghosts and he said why do you want me? But Josh was not scare but Karen was crying on Jeff shoulder and said our son will die because he saves us.

Jeff said no he will not die, about what happened 10 years ago it will not happen again, well they need five and Josh is only one and that will not occurs and trust me, and there will not be thunder storm tonight so he will be fine. But Karen and Jeff stood out and waited until morning and Karen was really stress out and couldn't wait until morning to comes, and meanwhile Josh was still standing and surrounded and almost taken by the evil one but the sun came out and they were gone and the doors open and Jeff and Karen when inside and Josh was confuse and mix up and didn't remember what happen that night. Josh said what going on? We will explains later, fine and Josh when into his room and his bed was upside down and the chair toward the walls.

The house was like spider webs and black flies were everywhere in the house and Karen and Jeff we cannot stayed here, yes we are staying and the ghosts are not going to scare us away and Josh will be control by any ghost, we need to beat it now, so just wait for them to come to us? No, we will win the battle and the ghosts will not. But you have not been drag to the ceiling and then they drop, be quiet, don't sees them, the shadows, yes, they are in our room, and about Josh, I don't where he is? He need to stayed with us now because he is fragile, I know, then Josh walk in and said we should have left, because I feel the chill and don't sees the frostily windows and then the activity began and the doors and windows closing and opening and then they saw the dark shadow and it approach Jeff and Karen and at that moment it slapped Karen on her face and push Jeff on the ground and stomp him very hard and then the door close and it was close and meanwhile in the library, the table and chair were twirl and then the books were off the bookcases and then it a appear and then it was like a globe and then Josh when into the library and the door slams tight and unable to open and then Josh saw the five and at this point he didn't know what to do but Josh was trap with the dead.

Josh looked around and went to the door and then tries to open and then he got poke and push to the floor and then got scratch all over his body and then he felt behind his head and then he was knock out and woke up the next morning and he still didn't remember what happen last night.

But Josh didn't tells his parents about what happened but he try to hide his scratch and bruises, but Karen said you need to get ready for school, and Josh said sure, I will be late from practice today, that fine.

But Jeff said I am going on a business trip and will you be fine alone until Josh come from school? Sure why not?

Later went they left, Karen decided to take a shower and when into the bathroom and step inside and Karen took off her towel and the water running and about a minute later the water turned into blood.

No, it happened again and now Karen tried to open the shower door.

# NIGHTMARE BEGINS

Karen panic and try to open but then she saw them in the shower and she said what do you want from me, I have not harm you, and please leave me alone, but then the lights flicker and the doors were opening and closing and but Karen still try to get out but she was trapped, and meanwhile Josh had a feeling that something was wrong at home so he left practice and hurried to get home, but on the way he had difficult to get home, there was a moment that he fell from the hill and slide down toward the water, and almost fell in.

Josh climbed out and hurried to the house and he had a bad feeling that his family was not safe from the ghosts and Josh knew that they wanted him, but Josh knew that he didn't wants to died neither, soon has Josh came to the house and Josh was surround by the five ghosts and he knew that he has to stop the activity to continue , and he knew that he had to be strong to beat the ghosts, but Josh still had the nightmare and still his dad didn't believe him, so Josh kept to himself and Karen knew that she have to save her son.

But the nightmare were getting worst and Karen couldn't explains to Jeff because he didn't believe in ghosts, until one night it happened to him and he was pushed and drag on the floor and bitten. Suddenly the radio when on and then the TV and the doors and the windows open and they were not and then Jeff, said probably seeing things and then he was knocked down to the basement and they were staring at him and one them had a knife point his heart, and Jeff was begging for his life and but

20

they didn't listen to him and then Jeff woke up and he was in his bed and he was relief and then he saw one sitting on his bed and he wanted to wake up Karen and then it was gone.

But he had the smell of smoke in the air that he was not alone and now he knew that Josh was telling the truth, and they needed to gets help to get rid of the ghosts, and then Karen woke up and said what wrong honey? Nothing and she lay her head on the pillow and then she felt someone was in the room and she was afraid, and heard a voice saying get out of my house.

Meanwhile Josh was quiet in his room and then they all came to the room and torch Josh and he was beaten and punches around, by the poltergeist and wanted to pull him into the basement and Josh had to fight it every night.

But then Karen heard the sounds coming out of Josh bedroom and she tried to go inside and it were not let her in and Jeff got up and when to the hall way and they were just stuck there and unable to get Josh out. Josh was screaming for his life and somehow they open the door and grab him but then Josh stay still. But the nightmare were not end and they had to save their son Josh, Karen said we need to get Father Frank back to bless the house now.

But the flies and cockroaches were taking control and the ghosts were getting stronger and Karen said we will lose our son if we don't help him.

I don't know what do? We need to pray and get this evil out of the house and you mean the poltergeist out of the house and I sees black shadow and then I sees poltergeist and shadows peoples in our home.

Jeff I will called Father Frank and tells him to bless this house and then Karen said we need like paranormal to comes like Josh suggest and we didn't listen to him, well I thought he was making up the whole story but now I know that is it true and I believe that we need now, about time that you listen to him.

Meanwhile when Jeff try to make a called it were not work and he was worry to tell Karen that there worst nightmare is happening for real and they do have ghosts in the house and even though Friday 13th past and the activity is very strong and it is just a force that cannot be stop by pray alone.

Once again Jeff dials out to make a called and the phone went dead.

Then he heard like a deep voice speaking to him and he didn't want to be in the room alone, if we do leave they will follow us, is that true Josh? Yes that is true, dad, well we need to defeated them in the house and then Josh said your crazy dad, what? It is a serious matter and we should just leave the house now.

I will not be chase out of the house, well dad it could be your funeral. Stop it. I have enough of this, I am going back to bed they will be sitting there, no they won't Josh look into his room and they were there standing and waiting for him and Josh said I am leaving the house tonight, where will you go, silent.

Josh step out of the house and looks around and then he went back inside and seat on the couch and was silent.

Karen when up to Josh and said on again you are sleepwalking, you need to stop that Josh but he didn't say a word.

Then Karen walk him into his bedroom and turn off the light and when to sleep and about 3 am Karen heard a scream and she got up in the hurried and ran into Josh room and he was laying on the floor and was torn and bitten and bleeding. Whisper and the voices and the pulling off the bed and someone sitting on the edge of bed, and hearing the voice saying yours not leaving this place and Josh was terrify but didn't says what was happening to him, and it was really getting bad and Josh didn't handle the nightmare that he was having and he didn't want live anymore, it was too much stress and he was planning to not comes back from school and just runway and but then he was worried about his parents about staying in that haunting house. Well Josh thought about to going to the library about looked up the history and event of the house and needed to know how to get rid of the poltergeist but then he thought well I am just a teenager boy and I cannot it alone.

But knew that his parents had some occurs in the house but they don't believe it yet, Josh needed to convince them to move out.

But also needed to have some kind of evidence that they have ghosts in the house, so Josh asked one of his friend to helped him to flush out the ghosts and his friend said are you nuts? No his friend Joe said you know who you are dealing with and Josh said I don't want nothing to happen to anyone and Joe said you did harm to yourself and you are making up stories to gets a attention, no I am not.

Later that night Josh and Joe decided to do a séance, but Josh mom and dad didn't know what he was up too.

But Joe said I don't think that a good idea about a séance, well I do, don't you remember what happened at the last séance, don't reminder me about the death in the house, well the séance that when wrong, well you can says that's so I am.

Josh thought about it and said I am going do it, and you are here at 8pm tonight, fine I will but hope it will not be tragedy? Stop this I don't want to hear no negative, I am trying, okay! But Joe was not too happy to go along with the séance and had a bad feeling, but still to plan to help his friend.

Then Joe said I have to go and sees you at 8pm good yes, and then left Josh and Josh walks though the path and he knew that he was not alone.

Then the alarm when off and Josh got up and he didn't know that, last night was the séance and he had like loss of memory and he walk by the library and seem like it was not the same but then step inside the dining room table was upside down and he saw Joe cap on the chair and Josh said did Joe comes over and Josh said it didn't happen, did it?

Now Josh was confused and daze and he asked his mom and dad did Joe come over last night I don't remember? Josh dad said yes he did and you both when into the library and you just came out alone.

# GHOSTLY WHISPERER

Josh went into the library and I thought he heard his friend Joe but now Josh was hearing voices often and they were in the same room and Josh didn't know what to do but he couldn't find his friend Joe and think that he might be dead.

But Josh think to himself and how is it possible, was Joe in the house, Joe told me that he would never step inside this house, I think that Joe is just hiding out from, I don't think anything happened last night, but Josh was a bit confuse. Did I harm him? I don't remember what happened that night and I just want to know, and someone tap his shoulder and Josh said someone is in the room right, don't you feel it, no Josh I don't, you are under stress and you think it is real but it is not. Come on my mom we are not alone in this house so I think that we have ghosts in the house, well we don't they were only incident, of what? Explains to me, well this house is old and it might be creepy but there are no ghosts in this house, well what happened when you would on the ceiling? I cannot explain but I just probably had episodes of what?

But Josh tried explains that he was seeing things and it was the dead, meanwhile his dad was away on business and Karen said well we will be fine.

I don't understand mom but we do have ghosts and don't denied it, I am not.

Later that night Josh was push into the basement and Karen was taking the shower and then suddenly she was wrap up in the curtain and unable to get out and Josh was locked up in the basement and surrounded by the ghosts and then Josh tried to escape but they were not let him go and Karen started to scream, Josh I need you help me, where are you and nothing, and about a minute later somehow Karen got out of the curtain and ran out of bathroom and ran downstairs and looked for Josh, where are you Josh? Nothing.

Josh staring at those beaming eyes and they were not let leave the basement but somehow his mom open the door and then felt the breeze when through her body and grab Josh and took him out and Josh like lost his breathe and that moment Karen felt that she were have to do CPR and she lose her son but she gave her breathe and he almost loss conscience and something happened and Josh and Karen left the house and when to the hotel and the middle of the night Jeff came home to a empty house and Jeff thought he was alone and then he when to bed they surrounded him and two seat on the edge of the bed and they pull him off and pull his hair and he couldn't get out of the bed and he was trapped. Jeff didn't know what to do, so he was being torching by ghosts and how he was terrify and scare and prayed to god to be alive in the morning, I couldn't believe what I saws last night and I thought that they were going to hurt me and then they just vanish in thin air and they were gone, then Josh said I told you that I sees them and you didn't believe me but now you seen what I been seeing all along so, now what are we going to do? I don't know but we need to get rid of the ghosts that will harm us.

But Josh was seeing white lights and Karen was trying to waking him up and Jeff said our son save me and but how can he is in coma and he is not waking up yet, and I am very scare that they might have took ours son away from us don't say that's! but he is not waking up so don't give up hope I am trying not too, but it does not looks good for him right now, and then he started to choke a bit and then he was fine and Josh said what happened I wants to leave this house before it killed us all.

So that night Karen and Jeff and Josh started to packed their things and it happen, something just pulled Josh and drag him through the halls and then threw him down to the basement and shut the door tight and Jeff and Karen try to open the door and it were not open and our son is in danger and we need to get him out of there immediately, I know but I cannot unlock the door and meanwhile Josh was in pain and yelling and screaming, it was torture and pain and said to Josh you are not leaving this house you are in my family now, never said Josh, I don't too be dead, I want to leave this house now, never said ghostly spirit in a ghostly voice, you will never leave and Josh saw a lifeless body on the floor and now Josh knew that he was one of them.

One word Josh said went did it happen? I would like to know, well it when your mom tried to wake you but you didn't but she thought that your still living but you are not, I think you are lying to me, then Josh looked and said I cannot be dead, and how did it happen well you fell on the flight of stairs and you fell and you hit your head and you die.

Once again Josh looked over and it is true and now we need your mom and dad, no you cannot have them, and then Josh woke up and said mom and dad I am having nightmare again, I know so we need to get out of this house now.

Dad do you hear me do you sees me follow my voice and you will be safety out and Karen said who are speaking too? Josh, don't you remember to him, no he is fine and we are leaving tonight with Josh, stop it we didn't save him what are you saying he is fine, don't you hear his voice but he is not here! It was the night of the storm and they taken him from us and not is nonsense Karen he is not dead, don't denied his death, Karen said if we take him out they will take us too, Jeff said I am not leaving him don't you understand? Don't get so nasty with me, our son is with us, yes but we cannot sees him and then it somehow got dark eerie and felt a chill in the air and Jeff said he is here now, and how do you know that's I just know.

One hour later Jeff and Karen open the front door and step out and they felt the present of Josh and he is with us and then they heard, don't stayed.

Then he touch his mom and dad and felt a good feeling and Karen said well it is time for us to go now and never returned to this house again with the death of our son, and Josh said don't sees me I am standing right next to you,

Now they walk into the car and Karen said this was a mistake to moved into this house and now we have lost our son, because the city was not good for him but not it the worst without him, looked mom I am in the back seat and not dead they are playing with your head to make you believe that I am gone.

Karen turned around for a moment and saw Josh in the backseat, and said to Jeff said that Josh is not dead and now Jeff thought she was losing her mind but then he said Josh you are here? Yes dad I am here and I am fine, they wanted you believe that I was gone to keep you in the house.

But I have the whole story about the tragedy what happened that night.

They did have a séance but they also had a killer in the house.

Then what to the killer, well he got killed by the house and then the ghosts were the living there and they wanted us but we were strong because our love was strong and we defeated them, but I still don't sees you, they are using me has to trick you to go back to the house and take my body from the basement.

You are dead, no I am not, but I only hear your whisper voice, but dad you're scaring me, but I am telling you the truth.

About a minute later it just got silent and Josh was not there and Jeff got out of the car and went back into the house and Karen follow and the door close and they were all together and Josh came up to his dad and whisper why?

Did you say anything to Karen? No I have not and Karen when into the bedroom and got to change and then Jeff went inside.

#  SLEEP WALKING

 Karen woke up about 2 am and she thought someone was walking in the hallways and Jeff was in the bed and Jeff was snoring away and then Karen got up and it was Josh walking in the hallway and Karen didn't wake him up and then Josh went into his room and went into his bed but he was not alone but Karen saw a dark shadow behind Josh and but then left the room and walk back to the room and Jeff was not there and then Karen heard pot and pans were making noise and Karen when to the kitchen and thought it was Jeff but it was that dark figure coming toward her and then she got a tap on her shoulder and it was Jeff and said what are you doing at 2 am with pots and pans? Well I thought it was you so I just came down and you were holding pan in your hand, and then they heard a footsteps and she ran up to Jeff and hold me and then Josh said what going on here? Did we wake you? No the man in black he did, what are saying? I saw him once again and so he said that she was taking me with him, don't listen to him, he is confuse you and too killed yourself, don't looked at him and don't listen what he is saying! He wants you and fights it and mom I am trying but he is stronger and like brain wash and he tell me that dad and mom don't want me, so you close encounter with the ghost? No he know that you are not getting along with us so he is trying to convince you to join him, so why are you saying that?

Josh was having ghost encounter frequently the accident and near death experience, and how he is seeing the ghosts.

Because it is happening the day of the drowning in the lake,

Josh approach his room he felt the present and he just felt that they were so close and such a eerie in the air, and Josh was really scare that they were take him, but Karen said no one is taking my son the man with the black suit, I will save my son.

Josh went into the bed and fell asleep and about five minutes later they drag him off the bed and started to write on his face and body.

Then Josh started to get up from the bed and the door slams and Josh fell to the ground and then Karen ran into the room and lifting his head and said your sleep walking what wrong Josh? But Josh said it is the house.

I know that you hate that we move from Manhattan to Long Island.

But we had to move because your dad got a better job and I also I got a job in TV, I know mom, well go to bed and we will talked in the morning. Okay mom and he lie down on the pillow and fell asleep instant.

The next morning Karen when to wake up Josh and he was not there, and Karen yelled out to Jeff said did you sees Josh and Jeff said he is having breakfast, at that moment Karen was relieve that was nothing but Josh was really acting weird that day like it was not him, Josh did sleep walks again I don't remember but I did feel there present in my room and Josh said that we cannot stayed here, but why we have " Ghosts" living with us don't you feel them, and they are watching us, they are, believe I am not making up the story it is happening, sometime I sees that ugly face on the wall of my room and it not letting me go, that is nonsense, said Jeff.

Karen said you forget the night of some kind of activity in the house and Jeff said the house is old and it creak, so you once again skeptic? Probably I am but I don't believe in "GHOSTS" then he walk out and the room and when into the kitchen and sat down at the kitchen table started to read his newspaper and suddenly he felt a chill and cold breathe and then a touch on his hand felt like

29

he was going to get pulled off the chair and then Karen and Josh came to the kitchen and Karen asked what happened? Nothing but he just denied the whole thing and got ready for work and left the house.

Jeff just got into the car and drove away and Jeff drove away and makes the called and said Karen I will be working late and I will be sleeping at the office, and Karen said fine, and then the phone started to have static and then it just hung up. Josh got ready for school and Karen was going to do the laundry and the washing machine in the dark basement.

So Josh left and suddenly Karen felt that she was being watched by someone but no one was around but still put on the light to the basement and walk down and with the laundry basket and when into the room put the load of wash inside and suddenly had a eerie feeling that she was not alone so Karen ran out but being follows by one the ghost and it were not let her go.

But now it was happened to her and Karen was sleeping and things started to happened when she went to bed and put on the cover and she felt that she was trapped and no escape and now Karen was terrify but she didn't wanted to tells Jeff or Josh but kept it a secret but each it was getting worst and end in the basement and Karen feet were dirty and muddy and had no clue how she got there, one night the windows and doors were closing and opening , but one night the door came off the hinge and Karen called the police about the incident but the police looked around and said the door was torn off from the inside, so what does it mean that the intruder was in the house.

After the police left and Josh was not sleeping and Josh said we have ghosts.

# PARANORMAL ACTIVITY

I know that you're right that we have entity in the house and a poltergeist that could be a demon, why do you say that? It is a possibilities it is and mom don't you hears voices and footstep next to your room I know it happened last night and it almost enter my room, but it didn't, and tried to open the knob but the door was close and then it appear in the room and I was terrify but it just vanish and I was relief and so I fell asleep and when I woke it was staring at me and sat on edge of my bed and tried to wrap me in the cover but I escape, so I saw the lights flicker and then it got pitch black and I thought I was going to get attack by the ghost, but you didn't and tonight we will get some ash and bless the house again, but the first time didn't work what do you think the second will, I will tell you why I have faith and believe and that will not get rid of the ghosts, how you know that's? about one hour later there was a bang in the library and Jeff and Josh step inside and suddenly the door shut and they were surrounded and Josh said do you sees them? No I don't but I want get out of this room, I cannot breathe but the ghosts were not let go but Josh had an idea to get his dad out of the room to sacrifice him. But the poltergeist would not leave, so what do we do? I don't know but they will tried to hurt us and or even killed us, no they will tried to possession us, you talking about a demon and this is a poltergeist, but they still wants us to stayed here.

Josh tried to get out but was trap inside the room and was not able to get out so Jeff tried to break the door down but it were not move and Jeff was hearing his son scream for help but, Jeff couldn't save his son and so Jeff ran down to Karen and said that we need to called paranormal investigate too comes to the house but it is too late for our son, I don't wants to hear that from you we need to go back to the room and find him but he is gone...

No he is not he is in the room in the closet and we will pull the panel and we will pull him out, how do know it will work I don't know but I am willing to save him and it is too late, why do you think that he is dead. So how many attempts did we do and there is no trace of him.

I cannot believe that he is dead; I feel that he is alive but trapped in two worlds, you could be right but I don't know and I don't hear his voice anymore.

Karen went toward his bed and didn't feel anything but sadden and her tears were falling and but she didn't say that she felt that the ghost took their son away and they need a professional to help them to get there son back and they didn't know where to find that person and then the doorbell rang and Karen when to answer and no one was not at the door, and then she heard a voice saying " Help me" then the door shut and it was quiet, Karen when back upstairs and told Jeff what happened and Jeff said someone playing a prank on them, and Karen said no one is playing the prank only the ghosts in the house and Josh was warn and we didn't listen to him and now he is gone,

Karen ran out of Josh room and felt a chill on her neck and someone saying out of this house and Karen said let my son go!! Then it was dead silent and Karen was in tears and Jeff said maybe we should go and leave this house and Karen said no not without my son, he is not coming back.

Stop this I don't wants to hears that from your mouth and I know that he is here and I am going to save him, do you understand the man in the black hat and with scar in his face will not take Josh from us to understand what I am saying to you, I do but looked around do you sees your son anywhere in the house?

No but they must be hiding him, stop this don't remember the night of the storm, I saw today and he said save me, but it is too late for him.

Then Jeff said watched out for the entity to comes and walks in this house, yes I saw them but I am not scare of them, they wants us.

Karen said I will fight the entities and they will not win and I will show them my love for Josh and they will let him go, you are delusion if you that ways.

Karen walks out into the hallways and some the shadow of Josh and called out his name and he just vanished in thin air.

Then Jeff said you thought that you saw him but it was not him.

What are saying it was not him how do you know he was in disguise and pretending to be Josh and how you looked into his eyes and you know this is a evil entity that we are seeing, but every time that Karen wanted to save Josh somehow she failure because of Jeff didn't believe what she was seeing and each moment that Josh was close but further away from them.

Jeff grabs Karen and said I am not going to lose you because you are the one that I love and Karen said about Josh? Not now, silent, do you want to die in this house, if I could see Josh, so my answer was be yes.

I am begging you not to says that to me, I need you so does Josh don't you understand that he drown in the lake and we couldn't save him.

Don't remember the EMT coming to house?

# PARANORMAL INVESTIGATE COMING TO THE HOUSE

 one day that Jeff decided to called paranormal to investigate the activity of the house and sees if they have poltergeist or entities and Karen were like to know if Josh is in the house and Jeff said I don't want to know if Josh is here because I were have the pain and loss of him, and Karen said I miss him so much, and so I do and then the called came in the paranormal team are coming tomorrow and they were set up the cameras in the most activity room and Karen said it has too be Josh room and the library, yes and the basement.

So tomorrow we will be leaving the house and staying at the hotel and the expert will tape and the reading of house about the activity, but I want to be there I want to see if they will capture the ghosts.

You mean that you would like to see Josh and it is not going to happened so I think you are losing your mind and they will be using EVP to catch the voices and get it on film and hope that they will speak to the investigate team but we will never see our son again and Karen storm out and didn't speak to Jeff that of the investigate and she didn't wants to leave. But they did and then they got a called from one of the team and they had sees something and caught it on tape and the voice and they also saw the dark shadows and they said you have shadows peoples living in your house and they took Josh. So we will review the tape and we will also check the basement for activity, and then the phone when dead, it was silent and of the team ran out of the house very quick and didn't go back again. Meanwhile in the hotel Karen saw globe floating and then it was gone and she said probably was Josh want to be with us.

Then there was a blackout in the hotel and now they were surrounded by the ghosts and Karen said I heard Josh and he is here, don't you feel it. No I don't! What wrong with you he is your son. I know but he died tragedy and we couldn't save him. I know but is present is here with the other ghosts, and he is not alone but he didn't cross over, because unfinished business so he was young teen and he wanted more of his life but he is dead.

At the house they couldn't use the electronic because it drain out the battery and they had to recharge but it fail and but they didn't give up and they tried all night and they got more reading one of them got push down stairs and so I am not staying here and she left and only two were left.

Then an eerie sound and footsteps coming closer and closer and then got hit in the face and one got shove into the basement and was like surrounded by all ghosts and then he climb up from the floor and got up and walk up and then fell on floor. The black shadow came close to him and drag him and threw him up to the ceiling and then fell and Jon ran to him and tried to pull him out and the door shut and Jon tried to open it but it were not unlocked and now Steve was being torture and then somehow Steve broke loose and ran out of the basement door and meanwhile Jon called out his name and then no one answer and then Jon when into the library and there was a lot of activities, and he somehow ran out of there and refuse to go back to that house.

One of investigate missing and no sign of him everyone got one but one and the head of the investigate said I was the one to called him and I should go inside and found him and one of the person said it is danger and we don't want to lose you neither and the other investigate said I am too scare to step in this house so I am not going back because what to me. But I do understand and I will go inside and if I don't comes out in ten minute so comes and looked for me, I cannot promise that I will, I am leaving this place now. Meanwhile there were some activity in the hotel and it pull down Karen from the bed and it whisper that you are next be in our family and now she told Jeff and he said you are just imagine things, you still don't believe me?

Later back at the head Jon walks in and he close the door behind him and the lights started to flicker and the doors started to open and close and then a chill in the air and then the house shook and then they all were near Jon and said, now Jon heard voice closer to him and the footstep next to him and then they grab him and drag him into the basement and the furnace started up with a flame and burned him into a crisp. About ten minute later, the house lights were out. Then the door was stuck and then Steve decided to go inside but he was scare but he didn't wanted anyone gets stuck in the house but Steve was calling out his name but Jon didn't hears him and then Steve thought he when into the library and Steve saw the peoples sitting at the table and looking strangely at him and what are doing here? Then they told him to sit down and Steve did and by why are you over Karen and Jeff house? Still he didn't get an answer from them and about ten minutes later Jon walk out of the basement and upstairs and about a minute later he got pushed down the stairs and landed on his head and he was out cold and not breathing.

Meanwhile Steve sat down at the table and hold hands and then the séance began and Steve said I am paranormal investigate and I didn't know you peoples were be here, did Jeff and Karen asked to comes over? Then Josh whisper no, you will be just like us, what do you mean? You don't know you will be dead, stop telling practical jokes, now I am getting scare.

# JOSH IS BACK

About two hour later they receive that they left the house and it is okay that they can go home and they receive a called from Jon and so Karen and Jeff packed there stuff and check out of the hotel and they got into the car drove in the dark of woods and Karen couldn't wait to get inside and go to sleep, and Jeff had a bad feeling about going home too soon, and they were about a two minutes from the house and said do you sees the light in the library? Well I think one of the paranormal investigate left it on, I think so, then Jeff said why don't we go back to the hotel and Karen said no I am sleeping in my bed.

When they got out of the car the door open and Karen step in and saw Josh on the couch, and she rub her eyes and then Josh said I been waiting for you too comes home where were you too?

At that moment Karen didn't know if she was really seeing him and was he really home and then Jeff walks in and said hello, Josh and then he was not sure what he was seeing, mom and dad what wrong seems like yours not happy too sees me? We are very happy, Josh came up and gave them a hug and seems to be normal and then they heard a scream from the library.

Mom and dad stayed with me, we need to talked, about what Josh about my day of drowning, did I survive the ordeal? Tells what happen that day?

But Karen said no I don't want to talked about it and we are happy that your home that all it count. Karen was not sure what she was seeing and couldn't believe that he was home, and then Jeff think about it, cannot be Josh.

Then Josh came of this room and said things had been change and I don't remember doing it, but we did, but why? Then Josh walks into the living room and put on the TV and then it got pitch black and Karen said where Josh is? About five minutes the lights when on and Josh was laying on the couch and fast sleep and I will not wake him and then Josh turned around and water dripping from his clothes and then Karen said I will sees my son later and Karen when to bed and Jeff sat down and looked the TV and then Josh woke up and said what wrong with mom? Well she is going through a rough patch right now but she will be fine, okay.

Later that night Karen came down and she saw Jeff and Josh and they both were sleeping and about two minute a wind and the door open and pushed here out of the house and so she tried to get back inside and it were not let her in and Jeff got up and when to the kitchen to the fridge and he open it up and the foods was white and brown worms and black flies and cockroaches were on the foods and Jeff threw the foods out of the fridge and then looked out of the window and saw Karen and he called her out and he decided to go out and asked how comes that she was outside but they didn't listens to her.

Karen came inside and said what wrong Josh what? Nothing wrong but why are you so wet? But Josh didn't know how to answer that' and was silent, and about two hours later Karen started to hear things and Josh said don't go to the library, why I don't want to lose you, I will be fine. You know something, stay away from the library, promise me, okay I will.

What are you telling me that the house want us? That why Josh is back because Friday the 13th will again in two days, yes I know and the murder will occurs again and if we do step inside the library we will become the victims and it will occur every ten year and we need to stop it now...

But how Jeff, I don't know but we should leave this house now and leave Josh, no I am not leaving my son again.

You willing to risk our lives for Josh who is a ghost in this house and you are not letting him go to the light but just keep him here, yes because he is our son and we should be together but he is not with us in a physician sense he is in a other world not in the living, I don't care and I am not wiling let him go.

So you are blaming yourself because the move to the country from the city and Josh could have died in the street but he died in the lake because the freaking accident, and you are blaming yourself but it is more my fault so just get your stuff and let leave, you can go but I am staying so am I.

Later that night Karen started to hears mores voices but not Josh and now she wandering if she make a mistake for staying.

But kept quiet and Jeff just kept watching the doors and windows and then it got dark and the only thing that they saw was shadows walking the halls.

Jeff got up and Karen was fast asleep and then they heard a boom and then the doors and windows started to open and close.

Now Jeff heard a knock at the front door of the house and He got up and went downstairs and they were waiting for him he walks by the stairs and then he somehow vanished through the floor and then the next Morning Karen got up and saw his shoes but he was not around and the front door was open and Karen looked out and no one was there, and then she shut the door and locked it. Josh said well my mom you should have left has dad begged you too but he is not here and I don't wants to tells you this house will get you, so un lock the door and get into the car and drive off from here immediately, do you hear me? I do but I will be alone and I want to be, I am not going, please go!!

No I am staying in this house and you will not force me to leave, even though you sees the " Dark Shadows" lurking and trying to convince us that we should be terrify from them but we are not, at night they might tried to hurt us but we still stay and fight for our home, that has evil force that pull us off the bed and hears whisperer voices and the chill in the air and we still stayed and our paranormal, some of the team are missing by do the reading and cannot found them they just vanish one night of the investigate and have not been since seen.

Karen walks through the whole house and some of the equipment is place and recording and they left the house and told Karen they refuse to comes back in the house and no explain why and they didn't even speak to Karen or Jeff, about what was going on.

Suddenly it got dark and the chill of cold breathe and now Karen knew someone was in the room and shove her into the library, and she tried to get lose , what do you want from us, just leave us alone but it tried to hang her in the library and she broke loose and ran out, and the voice said we will not let you go , then Jeff said come to bed and she said hold me, and he came up and hold her and she was shaking and had a goose bump and was afraid to speak.

About one hour later Jeff left Karen alone to take a shower and Karen said don't take too long I won't so Karen put on the TV and then it started to act up and meanwhile Jeff was in the shower the shower curtain tried to wrap him around and he make noise and Karen ran inside and said what happen? I don't know but I got trap in the curtain and I couldn't get out of it, and when you cane inside and it let me go!!!

No one was not holding you that were all in your mind, because you heard stories and that creeping you out, no it is the house and the ghosts.

But Karen refuse to believe that the house is haunting and sometime Karen get a visit from Josh and still believe that Josh is alive.

Josh came to his mother you need to go now but Karen said not without you Josh, but Josh like to begged but the evil force knock him down and was not seen again but seen in few days but didn't speaks to his mom.

# SHADOWS OF THE NIGHT

Karen said I am not going without you Josh so and the shadow will not scare me out of my house and don't you hear me what I am saying and then Jeff said it a lost cause and we need to leave now before the shadow will trap us in enterable in this house,, so Jeff if you are afraid just go and I will be fine and Jeff said no I am staying to the end of it, and then we will be safe and not harm from the evil forces that are being control and we will fight it with our last breathe, so Josh said it will be tough to beat that evil one and will not let me out of this terrible place and I am doom and you cannot stayed here, I want to help and I am not allow to do so. Don't you sees them coming closer and they cause you harm and death, please go and then the doors and windows started to close and now it is too late, and the lights when out and they were surround by the shadows peoples and they were about to pull and Josh step in and push one away from his mom and Jeff somehow open the window but big black flies and on the floor Jeff saw more than a hundred of cockroaches coming closer. The foods was rotten and Jeff said what going on in this house, and Karen said well we have ghosts and we need to go now, I am not going to leave my baby boy alone in this house and Jeff said I don't to leave him but he is among the dead and he cannot go with us, Karen said I will never forgive you for moving into house and it is your fault, no it is not you wanted this house so did Josh and it pulled us in and things started to happened, yes I know but I wants to stayed, but Jeff pulled her out and she bite his arm, what have you done?

Then Jeff I didn't do anything you and why am I bleeding, it is the entity in the house and it is haunting us and wants us to stayed, wait a minute they wants us to stayed here? Yes and I am not going to die here and I am leaving this house and we cannot beat them, how many are there? I don't know but time is running out to save Josh and do you have a plan to save your son from those ghosts, no I don't but when the clock strike midnight we will be trapped here forever how do you know that? Josh told me and I do hear his voice and so he is still alive, I don't know but we need to find him, but we are surrounded by them and I think we have a slim chance to escape, I don't want to hear that negative from you do you hear me? Yes I do and I believe they are watching us and so we better do something, yes now.

But the door will not open and we will be trapped here forever and they stood and the eerie voices all over and they felt the presents surrounded them and Josh whisperer and said I told you and you didn't listen what I was saying and how you both will be here with me and the rest of the ghosts.

What are you saying and the bad ghost, grab Josh and threw him into the well and into the water and drown and this time Karen said I need to save Josh and Jeff said he is gone, so then she slapped his face and he push her on to the floor and she hit her head and was out cold and Jeff tried to wake her but couldn't and then Jeff was surrounded and was pushed into the basement and hit the wall and his head was bleeding and then he took his last breathe and then he died and Karen somehow woke up and ran to the basement and tried CPR and but it was too late and then she fell into the well and then Karen saws Josh and Jeff and we are together again, yes we are.

But then Josh said but we are all dead and we will be here in this house and so now what? I don't know but what? So we are in our house and we need to follow the rule of the man that is evil in this house and he will tell us what to do! I will not listen to him, you will have to mom and so Josh, so we stayed in this room in the library and said Josh but why the library because there is a curse on this house and we didn't break it but it took us.

Well I thought went we move from the city were be different it is but we are dead and we cannot even leave the house. But I don't understand you will so tried to step out and see if you can go to the car.

Karen was afraid that Josh was telling the truth and Karen didn't walks out and Jeff said I don't believe what you are saying and I will step out.

So head dad, so Jeff step out but the forces pull him back into the house into the basement and said Josh I told you so, well Josh don't be like that's, and once again, Jeff tried to leave he was block and Jeff said well I think that you are right and now we need to warn peoples not to comes here.

Jeff said will they find our bodies? I don't know dad but we are one of them, yes I know when you can walks through walls.

Karen said if was your fault by moving us and now living here but we are not living anymore and she just floating away and so Jeff follow me here and said wait for me. I am not going anywhere so don't give me order, I won't but we became ghosts because you wanted to save Josh and now we are a family and so don't complains I won't but I don't like what happen to us.

I guess this is our destiny and now we can say we are home, but we will never leave that true, and then Karen said I think someone is coming and how do you know I heard a car coming up the driveway, and meanwhile the medium was in the car and I know that I suppose to sees my friends Karen and Josh and Jeff.

# MEDIUM ARRIVES

Dana and Joe said it seems to be quiet do you think that they are home? It seem to be abandon and like no one around and then Dana said they probably when to dinner and then Joe said there cars are parked and they didn't walks miles and miles away from home and then suddenly lights went on and Joe said well let go inside but we should rang the bell, and then Dana said I just don't feel right so let go home and Joe said why? I will tell you went we are far away, because we are uninvited guests so I think we should wait until Karen called us, so they went back to the car and Karen and Jeff and Josh staring at the windows and Jeff said comes back, and Karen said I am glad that they left.

They got into the car and Dana and Joe sped away very quickly and Joe said something is wrong? Yes I think I should have a séance in the house and reach my friends; Joe said you think that they are dead? Yes and I been warn not to step in the house tonight because it is Friday the 13th so don't you remember the tragedy that occurs 10 year ago on Friday 13th yes but I thought it was just a tales, but it is not. My friends need to be out of the house and Joe said they are dead and they will be trap in the house and not after the séance I will try to release them and they will be able go into the light with the other ghosts in the house but it will be really risking and I can even lose my life and Joe said I allow you do the séance, yes I will and will help me to summon the poltergeist out the house that will not harm anyone else. So do have the strength to beat that powerful ghost?

Yes and I will freed the innocence, you mean the good? Yes that what I mean, so who are you going to take so maybe a someone that deal with demonology technique and so knowledge. Also I will invite some of friends that will have cameras and EVP and when we will be doing the séance so we will have some proof of the paranormal in the house, and we will lush them out of the house and find out what happened to Josh and Jeff and Karen, Dana are you sure that you are doing the right thing, I need to find out what happen to them and why? Joe thought to himself that he were not go to the séance and Dana and her friends are looking for trouble and he does not want to be part of the séance and it is crazy and you don't know what will occurs and will you make it out alive and now Joe you are sounding paranoid and so stayed home and I will be back by midnight and I will be fine, this is not my first séance but you really were not in a haunted house before, sure that shouldn't make the different and when I leave I will called you fine.

Then Joe said to her the road are dark and you might get lost and don't worry about it Joe I will be fine with my friends and I won't get missing, and then he said how do you know that you won't? I don't but this is my life and I need to know what going , fine just called me when yours coming home and so I will and then her friends came and they all when into her SVB and drove to the house into the woods and very dark road and then Dana said to one of her friends we will be fine but Kelly was a bit afraid too says take me home but she was stuck with them and they drove up the driveway and the paranormal investigate were waiting for them and then they got out the car and when up to them and Dana got the house key under the plant and open the door and it was pitch black and silent and not a sound at that moment.

Dana went to the switch and put on the lights and one big cockroach was on her hand and she threw it off and then it was like an buzzing sound and then the lights started to flicker and then the door slam and Kelly scream and said take me home and she step out of the house and then the door shut tight and Kelly was near the car and saw the car key were not there and she decided to open the door but it were not open and she called out to "DANA " open the door and give me the keys, but nothing and then the door open and Kelly step inside and the door close and then she when into the library and thought they were there and then Dana said okay it is time for us go into the library and investigate said we do have some cameras set up but not in the library and then they heard a scream and Dana ran into the library and Kelly was on the floor and what happen and I thought you were outside in the car well the car was locked sorry I should have given you the keys and she pick her up and walks her out of the room and Kelly ran to the door and it wouldn't open, now what? Kelly said I didn't wanted to be here and now I am stuck because of you, don't worry you will be fine and then the rest enter the library and they all sat down at the table and Dana said now we need to close the door and hold hands and we will be fine and Kelly said I don't want to be part of the séance so let me out, and Dana gave her the car keys and said go home and I don't need a cried baby here I need to focus and then my séance will come out fine.

Seem like you want to conjure a demon and Kelly took the keys and close the door behind her and went downstairs and about a minute later she got pushed and fell on the bottom of the stairs and got up and pick up the keys and when outside and went to the car and it was pitch black and couldn't sees anything in front of her and then she when toward the car and when inside and start it up and left and drove all the way home but she was not alone someone was sitting in the back seat and then her car hit the tree and she was passed out for hours and meanwhile back at the house the séance was about to start and then Dana said I have a bad feeling so we stop it is Kelly and she is in trouble and how do you know Dana, I just know and so we better find her and Dana said we need to use your Cadillac and so I don't think Dana and why did you let her drive your SUV well she was a bit frighten and that why I let her.

Now I have no way of getting home so you have to take me and then we need to find her in a hurried and I sees a lot of blood and so I think that she need to get to the hospital, Dana are seeing that? Yes and she is not alone so let go and save her, okay but I am driving, so hurried, and it was dark and Dana didn't know which way to find Kelly but Kathy said well I think we are lost.

No we are not now we need to take the right and then a left at the four corner, okay so far we are headed home and then Dana said stop I see something, then Dana got out the car and spotted the SUV and Kelly lay down on her face with blood and she called out and the rest of them took her out of the car and she was not breathing and Dana did CPR and Kathy called for the ambulance but she couldn't no signal and so Dana said we need to take her, we will not be fast then Dana said I will use my emergency it is Star power that will get the help will it comes on time, we need to pray and she will be fine, and then Dana said we are not alone, how do you know that's? I just know so let hurried and they felt a chill and eerie feeling and the ambulance came and it didn't take long and Dana went with Kelly and she felt it was her fault and then once again she went flat line and they woke her again and barely alive.

Kelly chance very slim to survive said the doctor and then she called Joe and told him what happen and meanwhile paranormal investigate the house and things started to happened and they decided to leave but they were surround and the door were not opening and Leo said to Mark I think we might be trapped here, no we will not be how do you know? I don't know Mark but I do have a bad feeling, okay so let pack and looks at the films.

Mark said to Leo let me check out the basement, but why we are leaving I think I left one of the camera there, so go and get it and I will be at the van with some of the equipment, okay and so don't be too long in the basement, I won't be so Mark went down to basement and suddenly felt a lot of cold and search for the camera that was not located so he started to go back upstairs and then he heard a whisper and said " go away" and he shook his head and was about to close the door and he was shove into the walls and couldn't move.

About one minute he was lying in the floor and they all were stand and staring at him and then Leo came and fined him and picks him up and said are you okay? Yes now I am so let get out of here now, and slowly they walk out and locked the door behind them and started up the van and left the area quickly and Mark didn't looks that good and Leo said well I will stop and Mark said keep on driving and so they did about a mile away Mark passed out.

Leo stops the van and tried to wake him up but still like in a coma. So what are we going to do I don't it does not seems good so we need to get him to the hospital, says if he does not get out of the coma we have problem than that, yes I know they follow from the house and they will torched us and they will wants us there and we are going let them get us,

Then Mark started to scream and he is out of the coma and he is seeing them and he is near death and what will stop this paranoid I don't know but we need to get the help now before he slip back into the coma and make sure that he doesn't fall asleep, but his eyes are closing and I can stop it, I know but tried to keep him awake until we reach the hospital, and the hospital about five miles from here, but we are going to take him, I know but so they lifted him into the car and Leo started up the car and drove very quickly and said I think he does not have a pulse, wait a minute don't stop just drive, fine.

About one hour Mark woke up and said I think I saw Kathy and Kelly calling, and Leo said you were dreaming, Leo skid off the road and he saw the dark shadow that was following from the house, but don't looked at it.

Meanwhile once again Kathy when flat line and they did the CPR and once again they save her, and it was close to death and then Mark slip into the coma and then he didn't wake up and Leo said we have a problem he might be brain dead, no I don't want to hear this nonsense and he will be fine.

Then the rain came down and there was moment that the car got stuck in the mud and they couldn't get out of and it is vital that we leave this area now.

But the car won't move and Mark will died and I know that but we are stuck and they are after us and we will get killed by that demon and I know so tried to get us out of here, I am trying my best and I feel that eerie sound and the cold chill and the loud thunder and lightings almost striking the car and the wind.

Leo got out of the car and said one of you need to push the car and they said no ways the storm and the lighting will strike, but need to help Mark and he is almost gone, I know but I think that we can save him.

But time was running out and they all were stuck in the woods and they were surrounded by dark shadows that didn't want to let them go.

# DANA ALONE IN THE HAUNTING HOUSE

After taking Kathy to the hospital and Dana decided to go alone to the house and thought that she would get everything ready for the séance.

About one hour later Dana arrive from the hospital and drive up the driveway and park the car under the tree and got her stuff and use her key get inside and walks inside and walks right into the library and sat at the table and thought that she will have the séance tomorrow night and looked around for awhile and then left the library and meanwhile her friends were staring out of the window and she just walks by and felt a chill and then a breeze and walk out to the car and then she looks and she thought she saw Karen. No you are seeing me and don't be afraid I will not hurt you, but you are dead? Yes I am dead and you need to leave this place now, if you don't you will be dead too.

I came to find you and I did and now I can have my séance and freed you from this place that you will not roam, well I you hear me and I tell you to leave now and you will not be trap in this house, I just want to help you, I know that your my dear friend but you need to go! I refuse to be scare of that evil ghost, well he is poltergeist and he is really bad and means and he will killed you, you are giving him too much power and I am going to stop these tragedy to happen again in this house again! Hope that you don't do it alone you will break you, I am not scare so let me do my job and freed you all this hell.

I have warns you and now I must go back he will hurt me and my family, but you are not alive he still have the power and he will hurt will threaten and we will be punish, comes on Karen you are not weak fight him, I cannot do it.

I don't understand I knew you has a fighter and now yours giving up, no Dana I live here and it my home and if I know there was a tragedy I were never move but something pull us in this house, and Josh was the one that wanted to be in this house and I thought it was good to get out of the city and I thought I were go back some day but now, I am here forever and I don't know why?

Listen Karen I will find out and I will get your family freed, but we cannot go back to our home again, I know but we will not be controlled by that evil ghost.

The moment that Dana spoke the poltergeist try to push her into the basement and was save by Karen and meanwhile Josh and Jeff wander in long hall ways and so Josh said this place feel like home now, I do agree with you said Jeff to Josh and meanwhile Dana said probably your right I should go now.

Then Dana turned around and he was standing right next to her and she felt the chill and the eerie and the cold breathe and was about to open the door but were not open but somehow once again Karen helped out Dana to leave the house and then Karen was gone and Dana was in tears, and hearing voices.

Dana was pull into many direction and but she was not able to escape but felt trapped in house but her friend Karen helped her out and was safe so far and the poltergeist didn't follow her and she got into the car and but the car were not started and then she tried a few times and she felt someone was in back of the car and Dana had a bad experience with that ghost and but was glad that she was not in the house, Dana was about to called Joe but the phone rang and she answer and it was no know on the line and then she notice that her phone was drain out of juice and now she had no communicate with Joe and all the ways home through the woods and Dana was terrify for the time and didn't like that feeling, and then end of the road and it was pitch black and Dana was afraid that she might end up in the ditch or end of the cliff.

Going around those curve and her car swerve and skidding a few time, because saw a shadow and it was really ugly to looks at and wanted to grab her and then she just stop for a moment the middle of the road and said a pray to get home safety and meanwhile at the house Karen when back to the basement and Josh and Jeff were sitting and said you got your friend safe from here? I hope but I don't know if no one follows her.

Then Dana started up the car and the ghost said to her I will have you and you will be back at the house and she saw his face in the mirror and about a minute later he was gone... now Dana was relief and looked around and it was clear and remember that she had a charger for her phone and she plug it in and about a mile away from her home, suddenly the car just stop and were not start and the charger was gone and now Dana was afraid and then the phone rang and it was Joe and said a lot of weird stuff going around the apartment and she said like what? Well the door bells went off and someone knock at the door and then the phone was ringing off the hook and I pick up and no one was on the phone, I think it was a wrong number, maybe.

I think I brought this problem to our home and I will get rid of it too.

Dana I know that you sees the dead and you speak to them and so you don't have explains anything to me I do understand, okay.

When she arrive home Joe was waiting at the door and said why are you here because our furniture got move and the place is like a disaster and I think that we should go to the hotel and it might be safer and Dana said no it will follow us to the hotel and we are staying, and you are not scare.

When they came inside Dana said I feel the present and they will not leave and I think that they want to go into the light.

I don't know at this point but I think I will go to sleep and it will not hurt you because it wants me and not you.

Joe when into the bedroom and locked the door and somehow Joe was not acting like himself and then she peek through the hole and Joe was like smiling and then he close his eyes and fell asleep and then Dana walk into the bedroom and got inside of the bed and at that moment Joe was sleeping deep and then she felt like someone touch her and took off the cover and moving her from the bed and she said what do you wants from me I can send you to the light and then she heard said I don't want to cross over and I like it here.

About half hour later Joe got up and he went to living room, like sleep walking and then put on the TV and then when he did Dana felt that something might happen and so about a minute later, he was being push into the TV and somehow Dana had a feeling to go there and about the TV almost pulling him inside Dana grab and pull him outs and he woke up and said what happen to me? You don't know? No I don't tell me, well the TV wanted to pull you inside, what I don't what you are saying? It did happen and I am not telling you a story and they wanted you, don't scare me with this.

Now Joe was like angry at Dana and then he said why did you go to that house and I told not to, well I thought that place were be a good séance but I am still going to do it there, are you nuts and looking for tragedy to strike you.

The worst scenario is that you are bringing them home and I don't like it.

Well you know who I was when you met me and it was fine with you so what happen that change your mind about my work?

My problem is that you are dealing with ghosts and you bringing them home well I see ghosts and I don't bring them and they are always around not a haunting house and they do exist and I cannot help it and then Joe said I don't want to talk about it. Fine and then Dana slams the door and Joe slept on the couch and the next morning Dana was planning a séance at Karen and Jeff house and on a Friday the 13th and Joe was totally against it and Dana didn't listen to him and all her friends were gong to be there.

#  "NIGHT OF SÉANCE"

Night of the storm Dana and her friends arrive to the house and Dana said enter and they stood near the stairs of house and the lights were flicker and the doors were closing and opening and some of her friends were freaking out and said is it a good idea about doing the " séance " the night of the murders.

Now they about to step into the library and then the phone rang and it was Joe said you need to leave the house now , and Dana said no I am staying and I am doing the séance now.. So her friends Cindy, Liz and Katie sat at the table and Dana hung up the phone on Joe said Cindy said why did he called? I don't know so now put your hands together and now I will close my eyes and tried to make a contact with my friend Karen, and I don't sees her coming through but a strange man, he was pulling her hand and she thought it was Cindy and then she looked and it was the killer and he wanted to killed them too and Dana said don't break the circle and I will make him move. Then Cindy said someone is pulling me and she said it is not you but that man.

Dana stop for the moment and said we can take a break and then Cindy said we will break the circle and it better if we just keep on going, girls do agree with Cindy? Yes and just do it Dana so she kept on doing the séance and then the mirror broke into tiny pieces.

Cindy and Liz and Katie barley escape from injure and so Dana said it is too late to stop and we just started something and now I need to end it. Then the books in the library were flying around and one got lifting and bounce on the floor and then they saw flies and cockroaches coming closer.

Get them off me and I cannot and I feel that I cannot move and what did Joc tell you, well he told me not to do it, why didn't tell us and we are in the murder room and said Cindy what? You want us to die here? No!

They all got up and tried to open the door and it were not open and now what?

I will get you out of this place I promise on myself soul and don't promise anything and the door was jammed and now they stood together and she went to the phone and it was dead and then she tried to open the window and it was shut with nails and it was dripping with blood.

Then Cindy said I am bleeding and so are you and Dana said no you are not he wants you to believe that you are, I don't believe what you are saying and he is making you believe what he is saying don't pay attention to him, he is standing right next to you, no he is not and then she felt the touch and chill and the eerie in the air then something was pulling her in and she was screaming and don't let him get me, hold my hand and hold it tight.

I am but he is too strong and you will let me go and I will died tonight, stop this. Dana got up and pulls her Cindy and look into his eyes and she fell to the floor and they couldn't wake her up and now what? Shake her and what I don't understand and I don't want to lose my friend to that monster.

Wake up, wake up, Dana but nothing and Cindy and Liz let do CPR and meanwhile Dana was seeing white lights, Dana walking the path and not seeing anyone in front of her, but seeing the peoples in the tunnel and they says it is not your time so go back, your husband need you and the family that you are planning go back before it too late.

Dana looked around and sees her friends stand on top of her and now Dana just somehow wake up and they said we thought you were a goner and then Dana said we need to leave now, and about a minute Jeff appear and said I will let you out and Karen and Josh came open the door and hurried leave now. So they ran to the car and locked the door behind them and then Dana said I left my candle in that room and don't go back I am begging you not too.

But they didn't see Katie snuck into the house and said where is Katie and I hope that she didn't go inside and I don't that's! Katie was inside and looked around and didn't sees the candle and then the door shut and she was unable to get out and they heard the scream and went they got inside she was dead and Dana called the Police and they step outside and waited for them to arrive and Dana said you guys you can leave no way I am staying our best friend got murder tonight in this house, and I will wait with you said Liz and where is Cindy, and she came out with a knife and her clothes were in blood.

Police arrive and Cindy for charge of murder and in handcuff and about ten minute Joe arrive and I thought you were dead. Dana it is not happening and it is just telling you lies, your friends are fine but something in the house really scare and Dana said the police are here something did happen? Yes they find your friends dead in the wall and they are removing them, then she saw Karen body in the body bag and it fell and it open up and said to her Karen to Dana, you were my best friend and now I am gone, and Joe said what happen she spoke to me, I know I just seen it in your eyes, and they took all the body in the truck and they house was with yellow tape and no one was allow to go inside.

It was a crime scene and Dana left home with Joe and her friends and all the ways home Dana cried and Joe stop the car and Dana put her head on his shoulder and then said we are going home, and her friends were in tears.

Half way home Dana freak out that she saw that man in back seat of Joe car and said he had follow us and we are in danger, and Joe turned around said I said I don't sees anyone, and then the car swerve and skidding into the tree and they hit the tree and they were all out cold. About half hour Dana woke up and tried to wake him but he didn't have a pulse and said come don't leave me and meanwhile her friends still were out also and she gave him CPR and her cell didn't work and at that moment she thought she loss him and he woke up and she smiled and was happy that he was alive.

Joe said what matter I thought I loss you and then her friends somehow wake up and then he when backward with the car and went into the road and they drove him but Dana just felt something was not the same but she couldn't put her finger that day.

Time when by and things did change since that séance and Dana never when back to that house again, but Joe and her friends were not the same peoples they were different but didn't realize that they died that night of the crash.

Joe was not around and her friends didn't calls and Dana just sees there image and so one day she when to the place that Joe works and they told her that Joe didn't comes to works in days, and she said what? That day Dana looked for Joe but she couldn't find him and she knew that he was in the bed with her and so where is he? Is he afraid to tell me that he lost his job but scare to tell her and had lot chill and eerie in the air thought everything was okay, until one night that she saw Joe in bed and said why are you bleeding and he didn't says anything to her and now he just seem not to be himself.

One night Dana got up from the bed and saw him tossed and turned and then went up to him and he was not there, and she called out his name and then he appear and Dana said stop playing hide and seek with me Joe.

But he was silent and cold and the chill and the cold breathe and now she knew that Joe was not alive and said oh my god what have I done too you Joe you told me not to go there and you warns me and I didn't listen and I am so, so, sorry Joe.

Then he when through the walls and he was gone and then she was going to called Liz and Katie and but then the phone rang and it someone on the other end but no one and then it click. Once again Dana called Katie and no one answered and said what going on and then Katie appear and said you didn't save me, and then Dana said I don't understand what yours saying, yours not dead, and Katie said " Looks at me" do I looked alike I am alive? You are scaring me, it is your fault that I died in that crash, because we got follow by that killer, I don't know what to say, and she was gone...

Dana said I losses my friends and my husband and now I am alone and what will I do? I cannot change things but then the evil ugly ghost came to Dana and said soon I will have you also, no you will not and I do not threaten me, but dear you should be scare, I am not and I will send you to the light, I am too powerful to do that miss, I will beat you. Miss you think that you will beat me think again, and about five minutes he was gone.

Now Dana was relief for a while and about 2 am the ghost came back and threw her off the bed but Joe came and helped her and said I will help you beat this ghost and he will be gone from your life, and Dana said I didn't want you to get killed in the process but you did.

About one hour later Dana was in bed and she felt that Joe was nears by and felt safe and then the morning came and Dana got up and then took the shower and at that moment was threw out of the shower and had a lot of blood on her face and couldn't believe that she was seeing a poltergeist and were not let her go, but she use some holy water and bless the house and now the house was clear that she didn't even see Joe, in some way she was sad and so just felt a slight presence of Joe and the smoke of his cologne and a little globe floating in the bedroom, and Dana smile and left the room and about two hours later had a knock at the door, and she answers and no one was there and then the second knock she answer and it was like an cheerleader and she said well I am selling cookie and then the phone rang and said I will be right back and about five minute after the called and went to the door she was gone.

Am I losing my mind , no I am not then there was an breeze and then the windows and doors started to open and close and then saw more shadows.

Dana stood still and said I sees you all and you don't scare me, so I will show you too the light and the most of them said we are not going into the light we are earthbound. You will be happier if you do cross into the light and they all refuse and started to try to beat her, and Dana fell to the floor and didn't get hurt.

Joe step in and said do you trust me? Most of them said no but some said yes.

# DANA RETURNS TO THE HAUNTING HOUSE

Joe came to her in the night and said Dana don't go back you will not returns, and she woke up and said it was only a nightmare, and I am going back .

One afternoon Dana decided to go back to the house so she packed everything in her bag and her stuff and put into her trunk and when into the car and headed to the highway and then couple exit she got off the old road and headed to the house and then drove up to the driveway and then put the car into parked and took out her stuff and took out the house keys and unlocked the door and when inside and she said it is really cold and she saw her cold breathe and a little eerie and silent at once and then it was a banged in the basement and then the front door close and Dana when into the living room and sat on the couch but she felt that was not alone and then she saw those flies buzzing and when to the fridge to place her foods and they turned to be mold and gross and she vomit and then she was pushed downstairs and fell on her head and woke up and he was staring at her and said you are not going to leave this house again and Dana said what do you wants from me I can send you into the light, well medium I am going into the light and I am earthbound.

Don't you realized that you are dead, then he was gone and

then Dana got up and when back to the upstairs and lit some candles and threw some salt around the room and then said a pray and it was chilling and very cold and then she saw some spiders got on her clothes and tried to remove them but they were not nudge but then Dana just use her hand and threw them off and then the lights and the windows and the doors were closing and opening and the dark shadow walk in and grab her head and spin her a few times and fell to the floor and was out cold.

About ten minute she woke up and it was Karen said leave this house, and once again Dana passed out cold and Karen shook her but she didn't wake up.

Dana woke up and said oh my head hurt and he was standing right next to her face and he pulled her down and down and down and then she landed into dirt and he bury her and she tried to dig herself out but her nail started to bleed and now Dana was calling for help and no one heard her and now Dana panic and scare that she probably might not make alive, and the dark shadow was getting more rough and now Dana was bleeding and it were not stop.

Somehow Karen pull out Dana and then the Dark shadow shove Karen and she fell to the basement and said I will get you later, and Karen just lay on the floor and couldn't move and the Josh and Jeff said don't inference with him, he cannot hurt me because I am dead so what can he do to me?

I think that you don't want so know so don't inference with again he will make us suffer, we are dead so I can deal with him so are both coward?

No we are not but you trying to save your friend but she could be dead too.

I don't wants to hear that nonsense about Dana is dead, look she is buried under six feet and dirt over her face and she not breathing and now he let those black bugs out and they will eat her up. Karen said I am going to dig her out and I will help her to get the hell out of this haunting house and warn her about the killer is a demon in the house and I want you both to help me to save my friend.

Josh and Jeff said you are on your own and don't boss us around we are not going to help you and we are going back to our bedroom and she said fine.

I will get her out and I don't need your help just go and leave me alone, sure whatever you says and we are going Karen.

Two hours later Dana was out of the dirt and she was like passed out and not awake yet! Karen shook her but really didn't touch her and Dana didn't feel the touch of her friend, and then woke up and said what happen to me? But no one was there and Dana got up and pick up the stuff that fell to the floor walk upstairs and on the top of the stairs she got pushed and lay on the bottom of the stairs and blood dripping from her mouth and head and she didn't move at all, and they stood by her and then no movement and Dana for days and didn't wake.

Five days later Dana open her eyes and looked around and said I must have slip and I was out cold, and but I don't feel the same has before, and now Dana was having out body experience and said no I cannot be dead.

Then she saw them and they said "welcome home" Dana, what?

I am not home I am far ways from home and Karen said well when it happen you died and no I am not dead? Looked at yourself and tried to leave this house and it will not let you go!

I don't believe you, you can believe but your friend, that sure but you are dead Karen so are you, stop saying that's I told not to comes back but you were stubborn and now we are a family and then a little girl came,

# LITTLE GIRL GHOST APPEAR

She was dressed in a red dress and white socked and black shoe and about 4 feet and 8 inches tall and said you don't remember me? Do I know you? Of course you do know me I got lost in the woods and I was never found.

Did that ugly man with the scar on his face kidnap you and killed you in the woods and I don't remember what happen.

With long brown hair with brown eyes and with glasses that were bend and broken with the struggle with the man and the little girl name was Angela and she knew that she was not alive but still looking for her home and so Dana said you need to go to the light and Angela said I need to sees my mom and dad and then I will go to the light, I don't know where they move with your sister Anna, but they did move and then Angela said I don't believe you.

Then she just tried to touch Dana and then she vanished in thin air and then she saw the chubby beard man with a mustache and bloody hand and was trying to grab me and I ran to the car but he still was around and I felt the presence of him, he was the one telling lies to Angela and that why she were not go into the light, and then for a moment Josh appear and go now!!!

Dana said I am going to save the little girl and your family to go into the light, we will be earthbound, and we will not cross over, you must...

Angela looks right at me and with her brown eyes and then started to weep for her mom and dad and then the eerie sound were getting louder and louder and Dana couldn't stand the sound and said why are you making that sound to scare me away and Angela said the bad man is coming and he will hurt me badly and he will hurt you too, Dana stood looks and Angela vanished through the walls and the chubby beard appear and looks straight right at Dana and Dana got very weak, and then Dana passed out and her friend stood and look at her and then Dana woke up the little girl stand by her and said leave this house now .... No I refuse and you will be sorry if you stays what Angela said to Dana, stop don't do it just go and I belong here and you don't and then Karen somehow came and said you need to go Dana, you will be trap here by the killer, I loss Joe and my friends here and I need to do something, Karen said you have to go now he been waiting for you too comes.

I don't understand what you are saying and her friend Karen had medium brown hair and about five feet and six inches tall and not slim but medium build and a nice smiled and green eyes and she looked at Dana. Angela came back the man with the beard is gone now and it is time that you leave.

At first Dana refuse to leave and then she saw the walls bleeding and dripping on the stairs of the house and sees more dark shadows and knew that Angela was protection her and Karen vanished and the house got cold and with every word you said the breathe you were sees and it was really chilly.

One more time Dana looked around and said good bye to all her friends and husband is that she will not see anymore and Dana saw them clearing like they were just in the room with her and Angela open the door and said bye and then the " dark shadow" came into the room and Dana couldn't move and about a minute later the horn from the car when off and that moment Dana ran out of the house and close the door behind her and Angela was like inches away from here, Dana didn't know what her fate might be by going back into the house to get one important item but she didn't step back and said blessed this house and soon has she said it, the house started some activity and it was getting bad and someone was trying to pull Dana back.

They all stared out of the window and Dana saw them and Angela waved at her and Dana got inside the car and she couldn't believe the man with beard in the back seat and Dana ran out of the car and stood for a while and then when back inside and he was gone and she was relief and started up the car and drove way and didn't looked back, and the ways home the rain came down and Dana was crying.

"Then Dana stop the car and the rain came down and she thought she saw Angela walking into the woods and Dana was about to get out of car and then a car swerve toward her car and Dana car hit the tree, and Dana was out for few hours and someone touch her and said "get out of the car "it going to blow.

Dana was having trouble with the seatbelt and it were not unlocks and somehow Angela said I will help you.

About five minute later, Dana was laying on the grass with the rain falling on her head and then she woke up but the car explosion and Dana was far away from the car and saw that Angela save her from being dead.

Angela left and Dana got up and ever since that night Dana didn't sees Angela and Dana was in a deep coma and they were not sure if she was going to wake up, and on life support.

Dana was not breathing on her own and her family came to visit.

# BETWEEN LIFE AND DEATH

 One day something happened that they notice that Dana was coming back but then it stop and they said I think that you need to remove her from life support, but they didn't give up and meanwhile Dana was hearing voices that she recognized and she was trying to comes back but the man with beard was stopping her and was being held by him and he was strong and Dana didn't know how to fight him off, and Dana knew it was not her time to died. Someone whisper some word and but they were muttering and Dana couldn't understand what they were saying and Dana saw the bright light and tunnel and someone told her to go back and she believe it was Joe her husband that perish in the house and Dana couldn't forgive herself for doing that séance in the house and a lot of persons got killed because of Dana.

That days the family had to decided to remove Dana from Life support and so one person can save her it was "Angela" but no one knew about Angela and now Dana was thinking of what a wonderful life she had and but now Dana was between life and death and Dana didn't decided which path to lead so somehow Dana was thinking of Angela but Dana didn't sees her again.

At that one minute that the life support were go off, they started to sees some change in Dana and but Dana was still out of her body and watching what was going on and then they remove it and Dana when flat line and they said save her and they were working on her about five minutes and then the doctor stop and her family said don't stop she is not gone! It had been five minute and I have to call it time of death and then something happen and Dana woke up and said what happen and the doctor was shock and Dana was among the living but not the same in many ways.

Now Dana didn't see or hears the dead and now she was not an medium and didn't hears voices or dark shadow and then Dana said what did you do too me to her sister April? What are you talking about and then they sedative her and she fell asleep and but kept dreaming about the house and was more drawn too it.

But Dana lay in bed and didn't says anything and wanted to go home and they said no and April said I am glad that you are back and then Dana just close her eyes and April said let go home and Dana will be fine, but April was not alone and Dana didn't feel anything present there but the coma cause a relapse in her seeing the dead, but April was in the elevator and was going down and was attack by bee and then rush into emergency and then Dana was sleeping, and felt like something touch her and it was April and Dana said not my little sister and she has to be okay! One hour later came into Dana room and we need to tell you something and she said what wrong? At moment she felt some cold air in the room and said where April is, sorry she is gone. No, no, it is not true, not my baby sister what happen to her? Something in the elevator and we was really severe and we couldn't save her

Then she had an eerie and ominous sound in the hallway and Dana got up and they said you cannot leave the bed and she did and walks into the morgue but not alone at moment and saw that dark figure man and then vanished in thin air. Dana said there was a man and the nurse tried too sedative Dana she pushed the nurse and spring from her hand and got up and walk out and they tried to stop her and now the door close by itself and they were terrify of Dana and she was not the same and was bitter and mean.

More ominous sound and footsteps coming closer toward Dana and said I saw the other side and you don't scare me.

Then the lights flicker and the glass shatter and Dana was not alone it was more than one entities surround her and pulling her all direction and no escape then she when into flat line and we cannot save her, and when Dana woke up she was in one of the bedroom in the house and Dana said what going on and I left the house couple month ago and now I am back, so how can it be here so what happened I didn't leave here, I am confuse. Dana looked around the room with flowering wallpaper and no I am in Joe and Karen bedroom, Dana was about to get up and then she passed out we are losing her.

Two hours later Dana once again was breathing on her own and her family nearby and then Dana woke up and said " I am in the hospital" yes you are.

Now she was getting an eerie sound and ominous sound in the hallway and then she saw that dark shadow coming closer to her. Dana screams and they ran into the room and said are you okay? Yes and then the dark shadow was gone and Dana wanted to get release from the hospital immediately and then the doctor refuse, that night Dana snuck out of the hospital and then got into the cab and headed back to the house and about one hour later Dana was standing in front of the house and was getting the key from the pot of the plant and then open the door and when into Jeff and Karen bedroom to take the tape out the camera and when downstairs and was surrounded and we knew that you were comes back and somehow Dana said it is not my time to go and she approach the door and almost got stop but then it open and she walks out and didn't looked back and walks to the main road and called for a cab.

# NEW FAMILY MOVE IN

The day of the move Bill was having nightmare before they were moving in and Brian refuse to go but he was force by his mom and dad and Ben said what wrong with Bill, since you bought the house he was having nightmare and he does not want to move there, because he said someone comes to him and he is frighten and it is not really and maybe we should listen to him, don't get paranoid like Bill, I am not but maybe it is not a nightmare. Ben are you saying that you believe what happened to him it is really and he is being haunted, come on it sound ridicule and I don't want to hear any more about ghosts and haunting, do you understand? Tonight we will be in our new home and we will be happy there, and then her husband Brian said how you know that we will be happy because I feel it. So the boys will have their own and we will have a library and then we will be in the west wing and the boys in the east wing, so we don't have listen to their music and so I am glad that I found this house and away from the city.

About two hour later they left New York city and headed to Long island to there new home and near a lake and Brian said it will be a good used of the boat and Star said yes Brian and it will be a nicer place to live and Bill refuse to go into the car and said I don't want move, stop acting like a child, I am a child and I am only 16 year old and Ben is turning 17 year old and we are moving on Friday the 13th and are superstition? No but the nightmares are the warning not to move, stop it and get into the car now, fine! If something happened to me then you will believe me, stops this nonsense.

You are afraid of change and that why you are frighten no, someone did visit me not once but a few times, don't you listens to me we do just we will be fine no we will not be fine and I think it wants me, you are very scare and we be fine, and meanwhile Ben said what wrong with him? Does he have brain damage how he acted? No but he is just afraid of change, and that all Ben and don't tease him and he will relax when we get to the house, he is making me nervous and I just want be there and pick my room and sleep alone.

About half mile from the house the car skidded and swerve to the left of the road and it woke up Ben and Barry and said what happened and BRIAN said I thought I almost hit a deer I think , you could have killed us said Bill.

Bill was silent when they approach the house and Brian said I feel a evil force and I am not going into this house, and Ben said come on Bill, and then the car stop and then Ben said did you sees that's ? don't scare your brother, well I almost shit in my pants, stop it Ben behave and I don't want to grounded you but I will if you keep on teasing your brother.

Mom and dad you didn't sees it, sees what I thought I saw a dark shadow in the window, and Brian said well I am not going inside and I am sleeping in the car and I won't allow it, and then they took there stuff from the car and Bill was not eager to go inside and Ben step in the house and said looks at the spiral stairs, and Bill peek inside and then he was drawn inside and then Brian and Star stare at the painting and this is ours dream home, and then a moment later, Ben said where is Bill? So I will check the car and no he is not in the car. Where is he? He must have gone upstairs, I think so he just vanished and I will look for him fine. Everything was quiet and no incident a occurs and Brian and Ben they had their own bedroom and Brian was not too happy about being there and that night Ben came into Bill room and said why don't we just snoop around the house and Bill said no I am going well you are a chicken and Ben decided to go first to the basement and then looked around every inch of the basement and then decided to looked at the room upstairs and meanwhile Bill just sat on his bed and put on the stereo and fell a sleep and meanwhile Star and Brian were just talking about the house and Star said I thought I heard footstep and Brian said your mind is playing trick and no first I will sees how the boys are doing, well you are like a mother hen so, just make it quick and I will and so Ben looked around and he was about to go into the library and Star stop him and I told you not to go there and don't you listen to me, I do well just go to your room and Ben said mom I am not a baby and you don't have duck us in, well I am your mom and just go back to your room, fine, so Star said goodnight to the boys and when back to her husband and said we do have a problem with Ben, why do you says that's I saw him trying to go into the library and I stop him,, but why there are a lot books that he can read, no I don't want there and then Star argument with her husband and now Brian got up from the bed and when to the guest bedroom and so Star was alone in the room and then she put her head on the pillow and fell asleep and so did Brian on the couch and the next morning Star got up and woke up the boys for school and then woke up her husband and he said I am not going to work today I have a stomach ache and I am staying home, okay so you need to called Peter, I will and he lay on the couch and the boys ate there breakfast and left the house to catch the school bus to school.

About two hours Brian got up from the couch and went to the basement and started to looked around and he saw a piece of woods was loose and remove it and then looked and there was another room and he was to call Star but decided not to, went inside that room and then he was surrounded by black flies and they were really big and they bite him and then somehow he manage to leave that room and he place the wood back and didn't tell anyone what he found and he nail it shut tight and when back to his bedroom and when on the bed and said to Star, I need to clean up the basement and make it into the office and work from home, do you think that is a good idea? Yes of course I do and then Star said yours really not sick and you just wanted to be home yes and be with you alone and what got into you Brian, well the surrounded and just want to be with you, well I am going shopping so I will be back late.

So can you just don't go and stayed home? Well I need to buy stuff for dinner and fill up the fridge and but don't you want to have some husband time, not now but maybe later, well I just rest in bed and when you get home just wake me, I will. Later that day Brian slept in bed and Star when shopping and then about two hours later Brian thought that Star was home but it felt a chill and eerie feeling with some ominous sound in the bedroom and he thought he saw a reflection and then it was gone and then he heard some footsteps coming toward him and then it was gone and about one hour later Star came home and all the doors and windows were open and then she enter into the kitchen and fridge was open and milk was spill on the floor and all the eggs on the floor and then Star called out to Brian and he got up from the bed and came downstairs and said what happened? I don't know but you were home and about ten minutes later the boys came from school and said what happen here and all kids said we live in a haunted house, don't listen to those rumors.

Bill said I told you I didn't like this house and I do want to move in with grandma and no you cannot go to her, then Ben said well I am going into my room to study and called me when dinner is ready, fine and Bill walk out of the house and his dad follow him and said come back inside now, no I am not going inside the house and I am sleeping in the car, no you are not.

Meanwhile Ben was blasting his music and doing his homework and then he stop and looked around then he sat listen for a while and then fell asleep and then Star when upstairs to wake him up and then the lights flicker and then it just blackout and what wrong, I think the electricity just went out.

I will check the fuses and then we will have lights again in the house and where Bill is well tonight he will be sleeping in the car, you let him yes.

I cannot find him anywhere well he is sleeping in the car once again and meanwhile Ben looking around and step inside the library and then he was locked inside and the door was jammed and he was yelling and screaming.

# TRAPPED NO ESCAPE

 Ben was inside the library and no one heard him yelling and screaming and he was really panicked and was out of control and about three hours later Star heard him and unlocked the door and said I told you not to go there and you didn't and I did put the locked on that door and you broke it and then Ben explains that the door was open and Star didn't believe what he was saying and meanwhile Bill didn't go into the house and refuse to go in and he had a premonition about getting killed and he didn't warns this parents and brother but they didn't listen and Bill didn't comes in for dinner or breakfast and ate all his foods in the car and took shower at school, at school they started to called him a weirdo, but he didn't care.

When Ben got out of the library he had a bruise on his arm and Star asked what happen and I didn't know what to says, so I kept quiet and now he knew why bill didn't wants to stay in the house.

One late night something happen and Ben was terrify and didn't wants to move and then he got out the bed and the bed started to move and Star came into the room and said why are you moving the furniture, and Ben said no I am not.

Star was about to leave and something grab her leg and were not let go and said Ben help me out and he just stare and she was being pull out and Bill had a feeling so he got out of the car and ran into the front door and ran up and helped his mom and meanwhile Brian was working late at work and the phone rang and he answer and no one was and then it click and then once

again and Brain was alone in the office and then the lights when
out and it was pitch black and he couldn't sees anything in front
of him and so about a minute later he got push down to the floor
and he was being hold by a force and he couldn't get loose and
but about two hours later, Star called and was worry about him
and so he didn't answer the phone and so she decided to drive to
the office and then she collided with a car and end up in the ditch
and they couldn't get her out and the car was about to blow.

Meanwhile at the house Bill and Ben but Bill was worry and
said I have a premonition that mom is in trouble and we need to
find her, what wrong with you Bill and then there dad called and
said I am in a jammed so I need to reach mom and Bill and Ben
said mom left to the office and she didn't get here yet! But she
left about one hour ago and Bill said I am worry dad and hope
mom is okay and Brian said to his sons to not to worry and but
they were very worry and then the police came and they cut her
out of the car and then flew her into the helicopter to the hospital
and she stop breathing and they did CPR and she was okay and
then Bill decided to leave Ben alone in the house and take a hike
into the woods to find his mom and he was about to the main
road and then the car when up in flame and at that moment that
Bill passed out and one of the police officer ran up to him and
said we need to transported to the hospital and then they said
was he in the accident and I don't know but we need to take him
and when fell down he was cover with blood.

Five hours later Bill woke up and he was in intensive care and
being monitor for his condition and so we don't know his name
and then they took his mom right next to him and they were both
out of cold and they couldn't wake them up and then Brain came
alone and said I want to sees my wife, and so we will take you
into her room and then he notice that Bill was there, so where did
you found my son, so he was probably in the car with my wife.

Sir I am not sure but your wife is in really bad condition and
I believe that you should called the priest and give her last rite,

no I believe that she will pull through, and about my son and I don't know but he will be fine.

I need to find out what happen tonight and I need to know everything, well we will give the police report and we will find out how the accident happen and then Star had a flat line and you need to save her now...

We are trying our best but I don't think that she will make it somehow Bill got up from his bed and went into the room where his mom was and then he hold her hand and the doctor was about to says it is too late and then said it is a miracle and she will be fine and then the Brian said what did you do to mom I told her that I love her and I needed her to be with us.

It is a miracle but don't counts you're blessing yet and it still go neither ways do you understand? Well I believe she will be fine.

Ben was sitting in his room said he heard sound from the downstairs but he didn't go there and he just stayed in his room and waited for his dad to comes home and then Ben thought to himself where is Bill and then he realized that Bill when to search for his mom and got ambushed by poltergeist and hurt and was rush to the hospital.

About two minute he heard a knock at his door but he still didn't open the door and then the cold chill came and the windows were like frost. The wind blew into the room and the poltergeist was standing right at Ben and Ben didn't know what do and so Ben got up in the hurried and the poltergeist grab him.

# POLTERGEIST

Ben was about to escape but he got caught and were not let go and Ben was screaming from his lungs but no one didn't help him out and he was dragged and was like up in the ceiling and then drop and meanwhile Bill at the hospital said we need to get home and save Ben and what are you saying, well Ben is in danger and I think that we better leave mom and save him and that is nonsense and your brother is fine, no he is not and so go dad and I will stayed with mom, no I am not going, I will and you cannot drive my car and so I will walks until I get home and save him front that " Poltergeist" will send him to hell. Bill tried to convince his dad to go but he refuse so Bill snuck out of the hospital and took his car key and got out of the garage and drove into the street and headed home but Bill was really frighten and scare and thought to himself I need someone to guide me so I better start thinking good thought to save Ben and who will save me? Well I won't be selfish, but also they will wants both of us and I will not be trapped in that house and I will also have my brother save from the house and we will not be haunted again and so I need to figure out how to get him out the house and then what? I am not thinking clear but he could be dead and then what will do? Bill kept on driving there were things stopping him to reach his brother and meanwhile at the hospital Star asked Brian where is Bill and his he okay? Brian nodded his head and said Bill is going to bring Ben to the hospital and then we will be together.

About one hour Star said we are not alone here, what are you saying that ugly man is with us and he wants us and we need to fight him, and Brian called out to the nurse and said my wife is seeing things and so I contact the doctor.

At the hospital started to cold and chill and you could see your breathe and Brian said you are right I felt something that my hair when up from my neck.

I feel the chill and I don't like it and I think that a poltergeist follows me from the house and he wanted me to die in the crash but I was save and now he is after our sons. Why didn't go with him and I hope that he is okay.

Then Star heard a voice and said "did you hear that's" no I didn't what did you hear? I thought I heard Bill calling out my name, well did he called you mom? No he didn't call out "Star" you need to leave now.

Meanwhile Bill was about one mile from the house and the tire got a flat and Bill said I don't have a spare I will walk until I reach the house and then Bill almost fell into a ditch and then Ben was really scare and terrify about what was about too happened, Ben was trapped in the library and couldn't open the door and it was jammed and they surrounded him and he also saw Dana and said what are you doing here? So you sees me I think you're dead if you see me, no Dana I am not and I will see my folks again and I will be out this house soon and then he saw Karen and Jeff and no!!! What wrong Ben? I think that you're right I am probably dead and my brother is coming to save me and he will die too, and I have to stop him but that must be your destiny.

Bill was about inches away from the house and stood there and saw faces in the windows and something told him not to step inside but Bill was about to touch the knob and then he back off and then his cell when off and Star said don't go inside come back to the hospital and Bill said no I cannot leave Ben there, but I believe it is too late, don't says that mom.

But Bill hesitate about going inside and then a car came up and said don't go inside and you will be trapped forever and then

Bill saw Ben standing near Josh and Josh came out of the house through the door and then that ugly black hair man and Josh called him dark shadow, and he is the evil one, go Bill you don't belong here and it too late for Ben.

I don't want to hear that I want my brother back and I wants to take him home to my mom and dad, and then Ben came out and whisper to his ear and said take care of mom and dad and I am fine, no you cannot be dead and I need to take you away from here and then Bill said let him go and I will take his place but it is too late and you left and we took him.

Bill was going inside and Ben said go now and push him out of the door and the house started to shake and some fire and Bill walks back to the car and Ben was looking out of the window and Bill saw his face and wave too him and then Star said to Brian I think we lost two sons no we didn't they both will comes and you sound sure but it not true.

Bill got inside the car and bucket up seat belt and started up the car and back it up got to the road and headed back to his mom and dad and about one hour later there was a head on collision and Bill was DOA and when they took him to the hospital and they knew that he was dead and Star said you should have never let him go alone, but why his brother wanted him and so I couldn't leave you but you should have gone by yourself and now yours going to blame me?

I will never forgive for moving into that house and now our sons are not here and I don't want to see your face anymore, are you crazy?

No I am not so get out of my face now and I stayed with you!

# SEEING GHOSTS

Brian walks out of the hospital that night and Star was sleeping and then she heard Ben and Bill voices and woke up and saw them standing near the bed and said well I knew you were both okay but they didn't speak and they were very quiet and then Star said come closer and I wants to give you a hug and then Star felt a chill and a eerie and ominous sound and they were not her boys and what going on why are you mad at me?

I was not the one that wanted to move into that house but I did like it and so did Ben so we move from the city and there known one in the room and Brian said who are you speaking too, and Star said to Ben and Bill, they are not here and they are gone they were here, stop this. But I seen them and you don't believe me, but I told you to go and I didn't want to see you again.

This is goodbye Brian and Star got up from the bed and locked the door and then they appear again and Star was happy to see them, and said don't go stay here. About one hour later, Star said to the doctor Bob to release her and he said okay and about two hour later Star was on her way to the house and wanted to see what happen to Bill and Ben and she knew that her friend Karen and Josh were there and now just looks once and leave.

But the house had different plan for Star so she walk around the whole house got her stuff from her bedroom and then when toward the stairs and then she got pushed down and said, and she was laying there and no one came and then she saw Dana and said that were waiting for you and you came and Star said well now I sees you all and yes and so you are all ghost in the house and I will be going, looked again, and then Star saw herself on the floor and said I looks like I am dead, you are no I am not still having her stuff in her hand and then trying to open the door and it were not open and then she looks in the mirror and then she was all bloody and dead.

Are playing a joke on me? Do we looks like we are? Why? Went you fell you die, no I didn't, yes you did said Ben and Bill and you are a ghost like we are, the house killed you, I refuse to listen to you and you are trying to trick me, and I will not fall for it, and she tried to open the door once again and it didn't open.

Then she heard Brian voice crying near the steps and Star said why is he crying? Looks Brian found you but it was too, late.

Then Brian walks out of the house and he couldn't handle the tragedy and so he decided to walk toward the water and Star said I need to stop him. Star try to make Brian hear her and said Brian don't jump in the lake just go away and live your life, but Brian was at the edge of the water and was about to jump in but he got pulled away from the water and saw Ben, and Bill and Star standing and Star said go home back to Manhattan, and he just stood and stare at her and the boys and then walks away and when into the car and drove away and half way home he cried for his wife and two sons.

Then a red corvette came by and it was a blonde hair lady and she stop the car and said is everything okay with you sir and she was familiar to his wife Star and then he asked her what was her name and said Crystal and that is a nice name and she said thanks, and said are you having car trouble? He nodded his head and said no, recently I losses my family.

Well I am headed to Manhattan and was you like to come with me? But at moment he said no and then he said yes and got out of the car and when with Crystal and what route are you taking? You will see when we get there and then he looks closely and said stop the car and now Crystal was not listening what he was saying and then he said to her, you are dead? Let me out and I don't want to be with you, looks at yourself and what do you sees, well I looks like I am still alive, well looks closer, and he refuse to do so and then so we are just driving in the road at night? Yes we got killed on the road and then I don't remember that's so do you want me to show you, you might be tricking me to be believing a lie, but you are for really, really dead and so I am taking you to your destiny, he had a dark hair and slim shape and she just kept on looking at him and then she stop and swerve almost into the tree and said I was just playing with you and I am not dead and we are headed to Manhattan and I am going to the Halloween party and you are welcome to come with me and I don't like what prank that you played. Sorry mister but we could have been killed if I didn't stop on my brakes so we are fine.

About a minute later said to her did you sees that shadow on the road, well Brian now you are freaking me out maybe I should let you out of my car and so you can joke around about those spook on your own and I don't believe in ghosts, well if it is it is not my business, and she started up the car and said get out of my car now, you will leave me abandon in the woods and how will I get home, well that is your problem and Brian begged and said I won't scare you again and so okay if you promise not to be a jerk.

But he saw something but he kept to himself and then she drove the bridge and stop and now what? Your home good and he got out the car and she took off and he was stranded and he looked into his pocket for change and when toward the subway and looked around but felt like he was not alone.

When he down the stairs to the subway and he saw a dark shadow behind him tend what I will run will it catch me and I don't know...

Then Brian stop and it was gone and then he thought he saw Crystal and what was she doing at the subway, and he scratch his head and said to himself I was must be illusion the whole thing, and then he hesitates and he approach the entity and said what do you want from me,, leave me alone and then Brian got on the subway and sat in the front and he was alone and it when fast and then suddenly it stop in the tunnel and now Brian was scare and thought maybe I should get out of the subway and then he sat and then it started up and it was running and he got to his station and he was relief but the dark shadow was not too far from him and so he ran into his building and got on the elevator and now he was seeing dead peoples in his building.

When he got inside his apartment the phone rang and he pick it up and said hello and no one answer and then he heard Crystal voice and she said you are not alone and you need to leave your home now, and he said but why?

You are not safe and leave now, well you left me and you didn't get me and now you are warning me about the dark shadow that might hurt me.

No, I am staying and I will not run way and how did you get my number and she hung up and he sat with all lights on and so he was talking to himself and then someone knock at the door and he first was not sure to answer or not.

But Brian did answer the door and no one was there and somehow he was relief but also had an ominous sound out of his door and chill behind his neck with a some cold like a freeze.

Each breathe he took that he could sees it and then it somehow knock him down and was on the floor, and didn't move and he was out cold and but sees that shadowy figure standing right next too him and then it lifting him and threw him on to the ceiling and then he fell down to the floor and now he was being torture by that ghost and Brian tried to be stronger and try to beat it but it was really difficult and then the door open and then Crystal came inside and said I knew that you were in trouble, so you had a premonition, yes I did and I am glad that I came, so we need to cleanser the ghost from your home now.

I will bring some candle and some holy water, well you have

been follow by that ghost to your home and it wanted you and don't be weak and pray with me, I am but it refuse to leave and now Crystal, said be silent and I will bless each room and you will not have that entity in your house never again, how are sure about that? I think so but now it really wants you and I am begging you not to give in, are you kidding, I don't want to be a ghost, I know but this one is a tough one. I cannot do it and it refuse to leave so I don't know what to do but your life is in danger and it wants you and I will not let it get me.

But it is strong and it going overpower you so be caution and you will be fine how can you says that's just follow the rule, I will and will you stayed with me? For now I will but not for long. Now Brian smell some smoke and some perfume that someone passing by him and said are they here? Yes they are standing right next too you, why can I sees them because you are not dead and so you are alive, but I want to see her again but you will but not now, you will see Star and Ben and Bill again! But I feel that they are really close and Crystal said they are and so we need to let them to go into the light and then Crystal said well I see Karen and Jeff and they are fading away and so I think they will not haunt you again, but you need to beware of that ugly man that want you and you need to fight it and do you understand he took Josh and his family I know. Brian didn't want to know about them standing and trying to pull him into that house. So Crystal convince him to put on the TV and just relax but Brian was a panic stage and didn't sit but pace backward and forward and was really not himself and then Crystal said well I need to make you a drink and Crystal looked are his whiskey cabinet and so it was really dusting and mold and then she saw a big black flies passing over head house and said they are here, and how do you know that well you have foods that is with mold and the TV with some static and the lights flicker and then you heard footstep coming toward you so they are here. Well what are they going to do? I don't know but so I will helped you too get rid of them, but I do wants to sees my wife and my two sons.

But you cannot bring in the poltergeist in and it will haunted you hurt you, so why were you driving in the dark so I will not tell you until we get rid of the evil one, fine but keep focus and you will be fine and about a minute later Brian spotted a dark shadow of his living room and said what do you want from me I gave you my wife and sons and you cannot have me.

Then Star approach him and he smell her perfume and she brushed against him and said I do miss you so much and why did go to the house and then Crystal saying she is saying that it was her time and Brian was in tears falling from his eyes and said I really needed you and boys and we move to that house and then tragedy of losing you and the most important of my life and then the lights went out and then the lights when back on and they were gone.

# ENTITIES AND ACTIVITIES

Brian looked around at that moment they were gone and now Brian was going to bed and about 3 am, and it started with the lights and then footsteps and voices and Brian got up and looked around and then he fell asleep and then the cover started to move down and remove from the bed and now Brian got up and looked around and about a minute later he saw a light in the hallway and he got up and open the door and then it was pitch black and then he went back to bed and then he once again fell asleep and someone touch him on the shoulder and he turned around and no one was there and am I going crazy and then the phone rang and he answer and he thought he heard Crystal voice and then it went dead. Then Brian got up and went into the kitchen and he notice the pots and pans were on the floors and then the chairs were move and he called out and no one was there and then he decided to go back to bed and then he put on a camera in his room and fell asleep and the next morning he watch the tape but nothing was on and he knew nothing was wrong with the tape and so he tried one more time and this time he got push and pull in two direction and tried to leave his home and he couldn't open the door and then about two hours later, someone knock at the door and it was a young lady in pink and said welcome to the neighborhood and then the phone rang and he said I will be back in two minute and he went to the phone and it went dead.

Brian went back to the door and the lady was gone and now he thought he was losing his mind but then he notice pink flowers right next to the door and he pick them up and took them inside and was about to put them into the vase and then the flowers were dead, and then he threw them into the trash and took them out and said no, what going on and then the car drove up and it was crystal and he called out to her and she came to the door and said I been trying to reach for hours and hours and you didn't pick up your phone.

You are losing it and you will end up in the crazy and you are not imagining anything and they are with you. I know they are and they want me.

I know that I sees it and your not saying that I didn't I saw that lady going through the walls and you didn't sees it no, you are flipping out and I am not so don't argue with me and now Brian once again sat and waited for that lady with the pink flowers to comes back,, but she didn't come and his friends are saying you are losing your mind since that you loss Star.

So Brian when to his bedroom and lay down on the bed and put his head on the pillow and then he fell asleep and about 3 am it happen again and he got up and use the flashlight and walk the dark hall and didn't sees anything at moment and then Brian went down to the steps and when toward the basement and at that moment the open started to open and then Brian looked around and no one was there, and then Brian shut the door and when through the kitchen and saw the fridge open and then he closed and then it open and spill milk to the floor and so Brian took the mop and swipe it off and it happen again, then he saws her again and he said what do you wants from me and she looked at him and didn't says a word to him and walk by him.

At moment he saw Star for a second and said come back to me and I missed you very much. Then she was gone and he started to cried and then Josh said you cannot stay here and you need to leave now, and Brian said I don't understand I belong with star and my family.

Then Crystal came from nowhere and said did you see her?

No but you should go now, no I am staying with Star and then Crystal said well I am going home and Brian said I won't stop you just go now!!! Are you sure? Yes.

About two hours Brian sat on the couch and thought about star a lot and just wish that he were sees her one more time, but then Brian thought he were just stay in the house and then it happened to him that he was trap in the house and was not able to leave and now he regret it.

Now he was going crazy in each room he search for Star but she was not there and then he decided to looked everywhere and so he when to the basement and found a room and decided to investigate and he just when deeper inside the house and was getting confuse and daze and didn't know which ways out and then when Crystal was driving on the ways home she decided to turn around and go back to the house and help Brian to deal with his loss and so she got to the front door of the house and the door was wide open and she step inside and walks around and then all the doors and windows shut tight and Crystal said what have I done and now I am will be stuck here with the rest of the entities and ghosts, and I will become one, and she was headed back to the front door and Jeff and Josh appear and said your home now.

Then Crystal said I don't want to be here but I just want too save my friend Brian and I think it is too late for him too.

Crystal said I am not going to died here and I am going to get out of here and then the evil face appear and said you are staying and threw her on the floor and she was out and meanwhile Brian when inside that small room and check it out and it was like a lot of arts and old picture of the 1920's and so the faces were familiar and it looked like his late aunt that passed way about thirty year ago and now he was not sure that he like what he was seeing and he just started to feel heavy breathe and it was not good so he left the room quick and then walk out of the basement and saw

Crystal and said what are you doing back at the house and she said well I had a bad feeling that you need my help.

Don't stay come with me before they comes for us and we will turned out dead here, so you know the history of this house yes, your late relative use to live here and somehow the house bought you and your family here.

Well in the 1920's they were very wealthy and this house have peoples working and they also got murder in the basement of the house and the night of the séance the one that were killed they revenge and killed one by one.

But I don't understand you're the last blood line and when you get killed the haunting will stop and it will be end of the curse that your family did and it will end with you but why didn't my friend died because of the curse of the Lord.

Stop this and it I don't stay and perishes more innocence peoples will die?

Yes and so you need to decided what is right and what is wrong and I know that I cannot leave you and I need to lit the candle, and have the blessing water to save you if you want to be save, if you can get my family and I will trade my life for there, I think it does not work that way but listen to what I am going to tell you don't do it and come with me, no I am going with Star and with Ben and Bill, about Dana and Joe?

Crystal looked at the time and said we need to leave the house by midnight, but why? I don't have time to explain but we need to go now .not yet!

The longer you stayed it will be harder to get out don't you get it, Brian don't you compensation what I am saying and if we don't leave we will never leave.

I just have to found her and tried to let her go into the light but she is capture by that evil force and he will not release her so let go now, and he just stop near the door and didn't move and she said what wrong with you? Seems like you are under trance and you are not moving, just fight it and let get out of here and he said I cannot go, you alone, no don't argue with me somehow Crystal mange to push him out of the door but she was stuck between in and out of the house and then she was grab and pull into the basement and but push down the stairs and hit her head and meanwhile Brian was out of the house and everything was close and he was unable to go back inside and he was furious and Crystal was looking at the entity and said you didn't want me.

# HAUNTING

You let me go and Brian banged at the door and then Brian saw them staring out of the windows and about half hour later the security person came by and said the alarm when off and are you okay but Brian never seen him before and said are you new? Yes sir today is my first day on the job and he looked around said the doors are shut and should I walk you to your car and Brian said no I think I will be staying, are sure,, did you know that a storm is coming and I think that you should leave for your own safety and Brian said well this is my house and I do pay your paid check and don't tell me what to do, fine!

So the security guard left and drove into the dirt road and then went back to Brian said are sure that you will be okay? How many times do I have to repeat me myself, and then he drove off and Brian open the door and it seem quiet and looked around for Crystal and no sight of her.

So he thought probably when to one of the bedroom and about half hour later he heard someone was moaning and he looked around but didn't sees anything at that moment and then he took a lantern and walks down the stairs and notice that basement door was open so he looked but didn't sees anything at first then he walks down and then he saw Crystal laying with a lot blood dripping from her skull and Brian bend down and said well I have too sees if she is breathing so he was barely alive, and he took out his cell phone to called for help but it were not work out of service.

Now what and it my fault that she is laying and with a weak pulse and so he put a pillow underneath and lift her head and walk upstairs and then he saw the man with long black beard and was about to shove down the stair somehow Brian hold on but didn't let go but then he when back to Crystal and said I will get you out and said you go and I have told the history of this house and don't let it catch because it want you. Run out now and don't worry about me. I just cannot leave you, he will be back, and then he felt the chill and goose bump and said I think I am surrounded, and she said you are.

There is no escape so you cannot hide they are everywhere in the house and they want us, don't you get it, yes I do but I am leaving you and then knives were being throw at him and then big black flies were buzzing and then Brian pick up a piece of bread then he saw those cockroaches on his hand and now he vomited on the floor and then ran to the door and it were not unlock and then he saw Karen and Jeff and Star and Ben and Bill and more came and said you don't scare, then Josh came and he was angry and no one listen to me and now I am trapped here forever and no one didn't listen to me and I am mad and then there was an ominous sound with a banged and the house shook and Brian drop the lantern and it started a fire and Brian said I am not going to burn and then it stop for a moment.

Then everything was being throw and almost hit and Brian bend down and then when to sees how Crystal and they were saying she will be one of us soon and you cannot save her, but Brian kept on trying and tried to pried the door but it were not move his life depend so he took a hammer to break the window and but it were not break, and then the wind blew and somehow the door open and then he looked and it was Crystal standing there and said I do sees you.

Yes are alive. Looked at me closely and what do you sees, well I can see, but then a second later, she was not there and then he called out her name where are you and then she came back and you just like vanished, yes I did.

Once again he walks out of house and he couldn't believe what he saw for the first time, and he said well this house is on the ground of a dead.

No!!! I cannot be. Also I saw the curtain move and I saw shadows through the window and I think they don't know what happened to them and someone can tell them and they will rest in peace...

But Brian was going toward his car and something grabs him from behind but he didn't see what it was and then it was gone.

Then he step inside the car and thought he was alone but he was not, that lady in white was sitting in the back seat and staring at him and with half smile of her face, and Brian was about to get out of the car and then she just disappear and was gone, he started up the car and drove a mile and then she was again standing end of yard, she stood still and Brian tried to passed her but somehow she follow him and Brian skidding on the road and swerve a little to the left into the stone, not didn't hit it. But almost fell out of the car without the seatbelt on and then his car stall and he got out and check is engine and it was out of water and so he had to go back into the house because it overheated. At that moment Brian step inside the house with the jug and water to the kitchen and got some water and it was really quiet at the moment and so Brian thought it were be no problem and then the door were not open and Brian try to banged on it and it were move at all.

Brain struggle about one hour and then he saw a shiny object flying in front of him and felt a little chill and then this eerie feeling was not good at all and he wanted to get the hell out of the house. But he was trapped and he tried to break the window and it were break, and it really got freeze cold and at that moment the lights flicker and were stop and Brian didn't move but he got punch in the stomach. Then shove into room, and now he was block and surround and they were speaking too him and said now we are the whole family that you came back free will and we didn't have to force you.

Brian stood still with a frighten face and was shaking all over and now wander if he was dead or alive, but was silent and then they said you need to go the lake and drown yourself and now Brian knew that he was still among the living and not the dead and have a chance to go back home and leave this evil place and Star begged him and said I want you to be with me and the boys.

Brian said it is not my time and I am not staying but you did comes back to get some water and that all and not to be in this miserable house and so Brian step out and thought they were not follow him but they did all the way.

Brian walk fastest and but somehow they caught up and Brian stop and looked around and he was surrounded by all the dead that just came from nowhere.

Then he said waited a minute you all are gained up on me and I think I should be the one that make the decision and I am not leave me alone.

Brian walk to the end of yard and beyond and they couldn't leave the property and Brian was relief that he was safe but for now long, didn't know.

Because he needed to cross an others cemetery and so he didn't know if he had to deal with more ghosts and he didn't see any reflection or voice and then the lighting and thunder came and he saw something coming toward him and he just into the bushes and fell into the plot and now Brian looked around and it was pitch black and couldn't sees anything at that moment and then he felt a hand that tried to pull him deeper and somehow he found a rope and threw it up and tied himself up and started to climb up and reach the top and ran out so fast and didn't looked back and then half mile from home Brian notice some scratch and bite marks on his hand and said what did happened and he was like few step from his house and when through the garage and then he was kitchen and put on the TV and took off his shoes and relax on the couch and fell asleep and woke up the next morning and still looking at his cut and bite and bruises and took a shower and then it happen, that someone was in the house and he called out and nothing and then the phone rang and he answer and it was Star and said why did you leave and then it hung up and it was static's and no one was there and the phone when dead and Brian was afraid to leave the house and go to work to the office and now he was seeing dark shadow and in the house and Brian said leave me alone and it was gone for a moment and then Brian stood still and like in a trance and don't hurt me, please and then he smell something that he couldn't describe the smell but it was like rotten eggs and it was such so bad that Brian vomited and passed out and found himself on the next day and did miss work and not feeling that great and so he just stayed in bed for week into a month, and grew a beard and got a bad temper and was talking to himself and then he saw Josh and said I know you don't I? Are you saying that I am crazy? No but you have change after living in that haunting house and you became a hermit no I have not.

Brian refuse to leave the house and not going to work and doesn't answer the phone just live in the house and his friends are calling him but he just let it ring, and sometime follow the shadows where they go and a lot time he see ghost and but they don't touch him and so he just sit there, but one night Brian got up and when to the window and he saw Karen and Jeff in the ground, and then he saw Star and Ben and Bill and then Joe, and said I have my friends here and why should leave, and then he saw the bleeding on the walls and the floors crawling with the big cockroaches and reaching his leg and then he just remove from his leg and walks out of the house and his yard was a cemetery and said I thought it was a house with a nice garden and I am living with the dead and love one, and I am not dead, and then he heard whisper and it was Josh and said leave this house and Brian said I am hearing voices.

When he enter the room and then it suddenly got dark and Brian almost fell down and hurt his head, and when into the other room and check in the mirror and he saw that old lady and she was about to scream and Brian said no I am not paranoid but I think that I am.

Brain walks in each room and then he enter the lock door to the library and he open up the door and it was the killer and he was going be the victim and Brian cannot escape that ghost because it wants Brian and will not escape and it will be the end of the residence of Lord, and Brian was stuck in that house forever and then house became silent and when it happen to Brian he didn't feel the pain and but saw then all surrounded and at the corner of the room and said " welcome" and he said I cannot be dead. But you are and you will remain in this house, no it is a nightmare and I need to wake up and be home.

You are home and it is not a nightmare and so I don't believe you and Brian looked around and everything was not different but the same.

# OPEN HOUSE PART 1

One afternoon there was an open house and a lot peoples looked around at the house and a lot of peoples were very interest in buying this house, and so they gave a offer and they it was acceptance and then they were going to move into that house and Colin and Denise said well I am not sure I like it too much but why did you bid on it so I was thinking about making a movie in this house.

I thought we were going to live here, so what are you saying that you want to move in and said Denise, yes I do and I like how this house is build and I will fix it up and it was be the nicer home around and we will have party.

We will invite guest and we will have a good time and we will love living here, so will the boys, are you sure about that? Yes I am and I think that we will let my mom move and he said no we will not have ours parents here, okay and so Denise and Colin decided to move to the house near the lakes and then once again he asked are you sure and then Denise said did you sees that shadows in the house, no that was only reflection from the outside lights and so tomorrow we will start moving and then said did you sees that white shadow, no your mind is playing trick, I hope that your right and then but why is this house so cheap and I don't know Denise to Colin but we got an bargain and so they drove out of the driveway and headed to Manhattan and tomorrow will be moving day and I will asked Laura and Lenny to help us move and that is an good idea, yes it is and so they drove through dark pitch road and head then she saw someone standing edge of the road and then Denise look do you see her and he said stop it and we will be on the highway soon.

On the ways home Denise said I think someone follow us and you are driving me crazy and don't do it again, fine I will be quiet.

When they arrive their sons came to the door and said why are so late home and Scott said well I need your advice with my homework mom and Denise said not tonight and I am exhaust and tomorrow I will help you and then Scott said who is that Lady at the door and then Coin said you sees someone and he said yes dad, who is it? Old lady with a hat on and old fashion clothes and then Colin said do think that something follows us to our home?

Denise said I told you I seen something and but Colin was still a skeptic and didn't really believe what they were saying and then he went to bed and Denise stay up and started to pack the pot and Pans and then Scott said are we really moving into that " haunting house"? I did check out that house on the website and it said the previous owner disappear from that house and never found.

Is that true and do you want me to show it too you mom?

I don't know about the rumors but we are going to live there for a long time and you are not afraid that we might vanished no that is nonsense and so let pack and leave the city behind us, and then she pack the dishes and her clothes and then Colin took it to the car and said anymore stuff to pack and then Scott was really excited and then got mad and said I will not graduation with my friends in high school so you graduation and so you can just leave to college and that is right and Long island is not too far from the city and I can take the ferry to the city and meet up with my friends, yes and then his brother

Steve burst into the room and said I am not going there and I am staying with Auntie Joan and then Denise said no your not.

No you are not staying with Auntie Joan because she will

be moving into the house and that is all you need to know right now and so Steve was a bit angry and refuse too go but Steve went to the car and Scott was getting his stuff and packing into boxes and mark them (Scott) and Steve was trying not to pack but Colin refuse his behavior said you will be just staying for six month and then you going to Yale and so what is the problem? Well I thought we were being living in Manhattan but somehow mom convinces to move to Long island.

I don't understand why? Manhattan was a good place well at the house I will have a studio and a lab and that how I can make more movies, and about our education and about the school in that area, so we did the research and the school are good and you will be advance with your studies.

About my premonition that I have sometime so don't pays attention and you will having them and you will not have the illusion well I am not crazy and I did sees the ghost on Park Ave, about few block away, I know so change of scene will help you too cope and said Steve and I am not nuts.

Then he got into the car and then Colin and Denise and Lenny Laura and Steve and Scott all went inside the SUV and drove to Long Island and the car was pack and Scott was sleeping all the way and Steve was like looking around and then they got a called from Joan and said was not able to come tonight.

Then Steve said I should have waited to go with her and Denise said no we are a family so we go together, do you hear what I am saying yes I am but Lenny and Laura said this is our first time going to this place and I have heard rumor about that place and so don't keep us in the dark and so every ten year there are murders and missing peoples on Friday the 13th, what are you saying?

#  Moving In

 You don't says that it happen on that day and it will be about a week of that date and so are frighten? But why should be so then Laura and Lenny kept quiet about the haunting house and they had a article and so they didn't show the murder that occurs and so how many peoples missing and never found and so Colin said to Denise it will be about half hour that we will be at the house and we should pick up some grocery and that small market and then they can tell us the ways to go and I am sure because I have not driven in the dark and it will be hard to found and then Lenny said I will help you out and we should be taken that dirt road to the house and then we will end up in the front of the house, oh I sees and just follow that light to the house and then Colin said okay and now what turn do we take? So now you take a left and then a right and okay got it and now we are about ten minute away, good and I want to have dinner in our new home and then Lenny and Laura said probably we should leave but you didn't bring your car so you are going to walks, no I thought we could use your car and Colin said I will drive you in the morning to the ferry and but you are staying in our guest room tonight.

But Steve and Scott had a room near the library and Steve connect his internet and at first it were not work and then it did and the computer had shadows and but was not sure what he was seeing but Scott slept in the room where Josh slept and he saw things that he couldn't believe his eyes and then he saw something like something was repeating itself and now Scott saw the killer and then he shut his eyes and then open and then it was gone and then got into bed with a flashlight and then put his head on the pillow and fell asleep and about ten minute later he was being pull off the bed and said stop fooling around Steve and then looks and no one was in the room and then he fell asleep and woke up at 3 am and he saw the shadows and footstep and eerie sound from the hall and then he heard eerie music from Scott room and he got up and said Scott stop playing that music and he walk inside and not CD blasting but nothing at all, and then Steve went downstairs and fell and bump his head and didn't wake until the morning sun in his eyes, and then Denise said what happen did sleepwalk again? No I don't remember, and then when into his room and when back to bed and but Denise said you need to get dress up for school and he nodded can I stayed home one day? No it is a school day and you are going, fine...

But the most of all no one didn't believe him so he just kept quiet and let the occurs happen and meanwhile he was the only have things happen to him and the rest didn't have no activities in the house that occurs so they said they he need to get some help because he was seeing things and in the past he had the same problem so, Denise and Colin discuss his problem and Denise really didn't want him to end up in the mental problem at this point they thought hear was crazy and Steve said I have crazy brother with a straight jacket.

But Denise didn't want the boys to fights so she send them into there room but Colin said we need to take him someplace and put him on medicine and so I don't know but I do believe him but did you sees anything? No I have not and so there is nothing in the house and he is just seeing and hearing voices and so he is off his med, so he need to get some soon, and I don't want him attack us like in the past and meanwhile Scott locked himself in his room and then when on the internet and search about the house and then the lights when out and he started to hear footstep near his door and then he yelled out and said mom and dad did you hear that? But they just ignore him but Steve said stop this nonsense and so I don't want no noise coming out of your room and Scott said your all going to be sorry, you are getting mom very upset and don't do it.

I am seeing things and they are scaring me so don't you understand what I am saying and I just want to leave this house, about one hour later a storm came through and it shatter the window in the library and Scott got up and looked around and then walk toward the library and the door was wide open and he was about to step inside and Steve pull him away and shut the door and said what are you doing, sleep walking again? No I just heard a banged and so I wanted to go inside and check it out and you know that we are not allow to go into that room but there is no harm and so why didn't let me investigate the room, come don't argue with me, and Scott left the hall and when into his room and he felt a chill on the back of his neck and then said did you feel that? No stop it and go to sleep, and he kept his night light on and didn't sleep and but Steve when into his room and said Scott why didn't pull the sheets off the bed and I am not scare and he just felt the chill and then he just went to bed and then about 3 am Scott got up to get something to drink and he when down to the kitchen and then got some water and then sat at the kitchen table and then he got pull down to the floor and then he got a lot of scratches and then bruises on his legs and arms and then his face was bloody and cut and a lot of scratches and went he got up he started to scream and they ran upstairs and said what have you don't to yourself, I didn't do it, don't believe me? We are trying to be patience with you but I think that you need help so you will sees someone, it is the house and don't blame the house and it is you.

Colin said he is just acting out and he wants attention and we need to talk to him that he cannot get ways with anymore and if not we will send him away.

# SIX MONTH LATER

The time that Scott was telling them that he saw things and they didn't listen to him but one late night, Denise when alone to the basement and to put the switch on the fuse box and she felt like someone was watching her and then she felt a chill and then Scott came to the basement and said mom are you okay? She shook her head and said no someone is down here, how do you know I saw shadow and then I got push, and Scott I told you when we move in and you and dad didn't listens too and I was trying to tell you about paranormal and no in were listen me until it happen to you now do you believe me? Sure I do and I wants to be alone in the basement alone so let leave and go upstairs and locked the basement door but ghosts can comes through the walls and I know that's and so what do we do, let go to Aunt Joan house and stayed there for few day until they come back, are you going to tell Steve and dad what happen? No I am not they need to experience it themselves, won't they get frighten, yes they will and maybe your dad will wants to move out of this house, I believe we should never move in.

Well the price was good and your dad wanted studio space and office and so that why we move and also better school, well it was a good idea but wrong house, you are right but I cannot do it myself without your dad, so I will meet you in the car and I will be right out, but hurried up, I will don't worry.

Now the house is changing with cobweb and dark and the room with bloodstains and seeing those globe and shadow peoples and they are living in our house and now I don't know what to do and one thing that we need to leave Scott if I do get trapped in the house don't comes back inside just the perimeter and you be safe but mom I am not leaving you behind do you hear me and don't be so stubborn so I will not but I need to make a called and so I will be right out but don't stall it is danger inside and so we need to go now.

I will not let those ghosts to chase us out of the house do hear what I am saying Scott but if dad and Steve comes back early and they will not find us and then Denise said to Scott I will leave a message where we will be.

Looks what happened the doors are being open and then closing and I think it is time to step out before the doors shut tight, so I read somewhere that we were be stuck so I refuse that scenario, I know but on my mom and so left the note on the desk and then said no I will called him on his cell.

Scott was getting an ominous and eerie sound next to the front door and then Scoot said they are here and they will not let us go, they are surrounded us and we have to go to the back door, but hurried I am and they looked around and a minute before midnight the clock will strike and we not be able to get out and stop this are you having a vision? Partial vision and it is not clear and then about ten minute they heard a car driving up the driveway and no they are home early and I need to tell them to stayed in the car and then Scott said don't the car looked different what do are saying, it black and it is not a SUV and it is an old car and I cannot describe and it is a bad sign so don't wait for them just go and close the door.

I don't like how you acting strange, what? No I am not but I am seeing what will be, no you are not, because yours not taking the meds and you are illusion what I am not! Then Steve and Colin came inside and called out and Denise said wait for me in the car and he said fine.

Colin and Steve walks in and it suddenly got really cold and chill and they could see there breathe and then Steve said we are not alone we have a presence inside, no you are acting like your brother and then Denise came and said we need to go now, this house is paranormal and I don't want to hear this nonsense and I am going to bed and Denise said why don't we just go to the Holiday inn and so now I am going to be spook in my own home, and Steve said what the harm well I am not going to pays for the hotel and then Denise said I am paying and Colin said so head but I am staying.

Scott ran inside and said the car won't start and it does not want us to leave.

Don't blame it on the supernatural so it could be the battery so we are staying fine, and then they all to the room and slept and Scott got up at 3 am and something woke him up and then went into mom and dad bedroom and said comes with me I have to show you, I don't believe this he is sleep walking and we cannot wake him up and he will hurt himself and let follow him where he goes, and is that a good idea? I don't know but be silent, I am not I won't wake him on the top of the stairs and the moment that she said it then he somehow fell down the flight of street of stairs and Denise ran down and looked at him not breathing and I need to do CPR , and Colin called for an ambulance and they arrive and check it over and said it touch and go and then somehow he woke up said what happen to me and they wanted to take him to the hospital on the stretcher and he refuse to do and then got up and when into his bedroom and shut the door and said now I am home.

Then Denise and Colin called out to Scott and said get out of your room and we are going to Aunt Joan house and Scott said I am staying and you can go but I am not, and then Denise when to him and tried to convince him but he refuse and just sat on his bed, and looked in the mirror and saw Dana and said come to me now, sure I will. Then he opens the door walk up to the attic and talked with Dana and she said you know what happen to you? They think you're still alive but you cross the other side and now you are a ghost.

No I am not, okay do something for me, go through that wall, am you crazy I will get banged and I cannot go through walls.

You don't believe what I am saying, I am trying not to think that I became a fixture to the house, well you should have gone before your dad came with your brother and now it going to take one by one you will never leave so in your case you will not leave, yes I will.

Scott hurried cover the mirror and then sat on the bed and then he felt hands on him and he somehow pull away but a second later they were on his flesh and wanted to pull him into the library and but Scott was getting stronger and he didn't let them get him and then meanwhile Colin started to search the house for the activities and he got the chill and cold in the air and then that eerie and footsteps coming closer to him but Scott doesn't realized that he is a ghost but still didn't sink in and he walks out his room like always and Steve saw him and didn't think that he was an ghost but just tease him and said you became a ghost and Scott said stop it and your joke are sick and he walks downstairs and so then he looked in the mirror and saw his reflection in the mirror and I do looks a little different but not too bad.

Steve said do you know that dad having a fit because you and mom wanted to leave this house, well I didn't know but where is mom in her bedroom and crying her eyes out, but why because she thought that she lost you.

I am here and we are together aren't we yes and we need to find dad now before he end up in trouble, yes let looks for him, I will go to the attic and you will go to the basement and Steve said well I am going to the attic and you go to the basement fine so you scare of cobweb and spiders? No that is a lies, no it is not, I know you Steve.

About one hour later they were all together and then the light went out and then they came back on and Scott was gone and

Denise freak out and said where did he go? I don't know and then Denise got up and when into his room and he was not there so why is he playing hide and seek? He is acting like a two year old; I know what a childish prank, stop complaining about Scott.

Colin and Denise and Steve search all night for Scott and no trance of him and he couldn't leave we would have saw him and now I am worry sick about him.

Then they heard whisper and she said I recognizes the voice and it is Scott and said help me I am stuck in the vent, what does he mean?

I don't but go and get him, so they both got up and when into the attic and he was sitting on the rocker chair and he called out and said you frighten your mom, but comes on and Scott just looks right at them and but didn't speak and then Steve said what wrong with him did he have a stroke?

No but since the accident he just acting different and the close called and CPR he is like not like himself, I know but dad let him be and then Steve was about to push him and then Scott push him back and then Steve landed on the floor and about a inch from the table and said are you trying to killed me?

But not a word from Scott and Steve got up and left him and then the light when out and no sight of Scott and Denise said I don't like it.

I am going to speak with him and you order the pizza and Steve set the table and I will get my son to the kitchen and about two minute later they felt a chill and cold breathe, and Steve said we are not alone and like smoke came into the kitchen and then Scott was standing there and Denise when to the attic and open the door and walk up the stairs and then suddenly she slip and fell to the floor and was out cold and then Colin said I heard a boom and then he ran into that room and saw her laying on the floor and then try to wake her but no response and she was standing right next to her body and then Scott came and said mom I am glad that you are with me.

Colin started to cried and Steve ran into the room and said she is gone and Steve said I don't believe you dad she is just sleeping deep no she is not here.

Are you should, dad? Yes I am positive about that she doesn't have a pulse and so where is Scott, I don't he just disappear and nowhere, what game is he playing, I don't know dad.

Then the police arrive and ambulance and took the body to the morgue and then this is sadden day of my life without Denise and I know dad without mom and so she was my life and so we are on our own and I will leave you to watched your brother and I need to do the paperwork for your mom.

But don't say anything to Scott because he will says the house killed mom.

# TRAGEDY STRIKES AGAIN

 Once again the tragedy strike one death occurs after Friday 13th and Steve just wander around the house and didn't find him and then he saw a secret door and Steve investigate and then the door shut behind him and he couldn't open it and he banged at the door and no one were open and then he heard voices and whisper and even his hair were stick up and looked around and then the black flies surrounded him and went right to his face and started to bite him and he use his finger and scratch the door and try to open it and he was stuck and then he was surrounded and he saw Scott and His mom and she pull him toward him and said I been looking for, mom what are you saying and then the water came and it was getting higher and higher and Steve said are you trying to drown me? But they were silent and Steve was getting really scare and said let me go, I don't want to die here.

Two hours later Colin came home and he was crying a lot and thought that Steve was in his room and wanted to be alone so Colin went to his bedroom and she was laying on the bed and said honey and he kissed her lips and I really missed you. You are dead are you drunk again, I am alive like you are and then he touches her and you are really here, of course you when out with the guys don't you remember, yes I do and you got killed by the house and how can a house killed someone, you had a lot scotch and so go to the bathroom..

Then Steve said mom you're here and I am happy that you are

home and she smiled and with a little twinkle in her eye and so Steve said say anything but knew it was not real.

But he knew she was just like her and his dad didn't figure out that they were dad and he was the only still living and thinking that everything was okay.

Colin said to his boys it is time for bed and you both have to get up in the morning to school and did you do your homework.

Yes we did and they left in a hurried and then Denise when into the bedroom and lay down on the bed and called Colin to comes to her and he just walk in and lock the door and when next to her and said well we have a chill in the room and but she was very quiet and he kissed her lips and then they make love and Colin and fell asleep and about 2 am Colin woke up and looked and she was gone and then got up and walks toward the library and heard a sound and stop for a moment and then open the door and it was pitch black and then he put on the switch and then Denise called him and then he shut the door and when to her and then he said where were you and she said I was in the kitchen and I just got some drink that I was thirsty.

Why didn't you answer me when I called out your name well I didn't hear you and then she called out Colin and Scott and Steve where are you and then she saw them in the mirror and said you cannot be there so get out now we cannot we are trapped and I am going to shatter the mirror and you will have seven year of bad luck and then Colin moaning and groaning and said help me I am stuck in the stairs that lead to the basement, and Denise said well I am not strong enough but I will try and do my best and I will called our sons too help and it seem like it took forever to get him out but somehow he just climb out and then Denise said, well, well you got out and then smoke was coming from the furnace and it got darker and darker and she didn't see him and when the smoke was gone she was in the library standing by the beard man with knife pointed toward her and she was about to scream and the knife when through her and it didn't hurt her at all and so he said yes you are one of us.

She reply and said I don't know what you are saying, well you do live here? Yes I do and I will be staying here and he maniac laughed and said you are not leaving and you live here all ready and I don't need to killed you because you are dead all ready.

Colin walk around and said well I better leave before the storm and I will take my family and then door hinge open and he walks out and it thunder and lighting and then thought I need to found my car keys and my family and at that moment he thought he saw Scott and then he looked and he was gone.

Colin when back into the house and now the lights were flicker and the doors and windows closing and opening and then he got push down and it was Denise and said why did you comes back inside and you should have left and I cannot leave you and I love you all. You cannot stayed and why not? Because you will be dead, Colin then walks away and then he pick up his keys and laptop computer and was about to open the door and he was unable to open it and he push and pull it and it were not nudge not a bit.

Now Colin was getting furious and mad that he was trapped in the house and Josh whisper to him the best way to escape through the library and then from the window, so then Colin went inside and then got trapped surrounded by all of ghosts and then the ugly beard and stood by him and grab him and push him down and went through the window and shatter and went down and fell to the ground, he lying on his face and not moving and Denise standing near him and then he got up and they both walk into the house together.

# GHOST HOUSE

Colin and Denise walk inside and the door close behind them.

Went you so by the house you shadows through window and walking around the house with a lot eerie sound and ominous echo in the house... walking and ghostly whisper from every side of the house and one late night Kelly and Joe were walking by the house and Kelly said let just keep on walking and so but Joe wanted to go inside and Kelly refuse to go inside and so Joe when inside and said comes on in Kelly don't be afraid. I am not going inside and I will wait for you outside, fine. Then Kelly looked and said did you see that dark shadow? Nope you are just seeing things, no I am not.

Colin and Denise sat down with the rest of the spirit and they chat and then they said that they need a good haunting and scare some folks out of there wit and Colin said well we were scare and we came back and that was totally a mistake and so now we roam the hall of this house, that we purchase and now we live her forever and they will never found our bodies.

They might found your bones, but nothing else in the dirt under the house there will be any trace of you. Thank a lot that I didn't want to hear but it is the truth so deal with it and I thought it were never happen to me but it did.

Listen, what I am saying we this is our living quarter and so that all I can says for now. So everyone has their room and when someone comes in we need to decide if they stay or not.

So at that moment Joe step inside the house and looked

around and then called in Kelly and Kelly just step in but a bit and then Kelly said this place smell of death and she walks out and then Joe looked around every corner of the house and now Joe know that he is not alone. But still peep in each room and fall into the hole in the floor and he called out and said Kelly I need your help and she run inside and said how can I help you? Pull me out now I don't have the strength, yes you do and don't leave me I told you not to go inside but you did, so you are going to punish me? No I am going to help you and then we are going home, fine! Kelly ran inside and looked for Joe and said to herself why did I go inside, but then search for Joe and then saw a hole in the ceiling and looked down and Kelly went to the basement door and open it and Joe was laying on his back and moaning and groaning, and seeing ghosts in front of him and yelling and screaming and said, I was so stupid to go into the house and you warn me but I was stubborn and I didn't listen to you and so try to pick me up and I will walks slow and then they reach the stairs and so they stop for the moment and then he hold on to Kelly and then they walks slowly upstairs and then they reach the top of stair and Kelly was relieve.

Then the house started to shake and move and Joe almost fell down again but he was holding on too Kelly.

But you are holding me too tight and then Joe said I am holding you so who is? I don't know but it is not me.

Are you sure that you are not; I know I am standing on my two feet without holding you. So who is holding me said Kelly I don't know that shadow with the chill in the air, then she saw his eyes staring at her and they were two red eyes and Kelly was scare and terrify at that moment and then Joe said I will count to ten and we will get out of this ghost house.

Will it works? I don't know but I am willing to tried, you but us in danger and now you have to get us out do you understand what I am saying too you? Totally and I do understand and I am sorry that I got us into this trouble.

So how are you going get us out and I am thinking and don't take too long and I don't want to dies in that house, I just want to go home.

So tell me what is yours plan to get out of this house well first we need to find the front door and open it and hope it opened. What will be our second move well you know that you need to help me to get out of the house so you will need a stick to help with your walking out but I will not be able to find a stick so I will help you by holding the best has I can.

Listens, and move when I move and then we will be near the doorway and then I will open up the doorknob and get out this creepy house. But Joe felt like someone was following them and he didn't says anything to Kelly and didn't want her to freak out and kept silent and then she got knock down and Joe said where are you, don't you see me on the floor? Now I do.

Suddenly it really got cold and chill and they saw there breathe and said we are not alone they are here, yes and we are surrounded, good guest, so Joe how do we get out and I don't want to be here, sorry about going inside and you follow me inside to save me. I should have, but you didn't but now we are stuck for now. I will figure out a plan and I will try to break a window but they got nails. I know what to keep out or coming in? Don't have a clue at this moment.

Then the footsteps were coming toward Joe and Kelly and stood still and they were afraid to move and Joe said we probably should move we are like sitting duck, don't says why with the smart remark, I don't but you do rub me the wrong way well bringing you into the house and I know but stop nagging me and I am sick and tired, just leave me alone we are not alone they are here.

I know and I am mad that you when inside and then I enter and now we are trapped I know I have heard that from many times, lay off fine.

I thought we suppose to stick together and now you are chasing me away, that is not an brilliant ideas but so leave I don't care I will get out this house without you, sure you will Kelly, and don't delusion, I am not you live in an fantasy world just like you.

Don't be such an pain in butt, well I don't like that we are in this ghost house and I warns you but you were a butt head and wanted too investigate and you stop, and think about getting out, then they heard a alarm going off and what does that mean, I don't know but they are coming closer and they wants us to be here and somehow the wind blow and Kelly when outside and so did Joe and said okay now we are safe and we are going home, and she nodded her head and said yes we are, and smile and kissed his lips and what was that for?

Just thanking you for getting us out and he said don't sees the graveyard the shadows lurking, yes I do so we just go to the main road and we don't go near the cemetery and we will be fine when we leave the property, yes you are right but we are being follows, yes we bought them out and now they will surrounded us, no ways!

About one hour later Joe and Kelly walks through the path and so seems like we are fine and no one is behind us so we will cross the bridge and we will be home soon. Yes and I will be there about ten minutes and so do you wants to come in? No I better go home now because my mom and dad are waiting for me.

So I will sees you tomorrow at the dance, after school and then Kelly said why so many black flies are going after us and I don't know and I cannot killed them so what are you going to tell your folks, nothing.

When Joe was headed home he was attacked by black flies and then he called Kelly from his cell and said they are going home with me and Kelly couldn't understand what he was saying the phone got static and couldn't hear him and then just disconnect and Kelly tried a few time and when to voice mail so I need to reach and so Joe slip into the ditch on the way after the attack and his face was all red and scar with bite and he was just laying on the ground.

# HELP!!! SAVE ME.

 Joe was digging and climbing from the ditch and once again he fell and hit his head and lay there and meanwhile Kelly was in her bed and was sleeping and then she heard someone saying " Help me, save me" and then she woke and said Joe where are you? I called you but you didn't answer and then she saw some shadow in her bedroom going into circles and what do you want from me?

Then it just stop and looked at her and just vanished in thin air and but Kelly couldn't explains what happen and thought she was just dreaming.

Then saw that shiny globe floating in the room and meanwhile Joe was like being buried alive so Kelly called him and but she woke him up and he was very angry and she said sorry but I heard you calling out for me.

About a second she heard a clank coming from her attic and she said Joe I will called you back so where are you going I have check it out, please don't go alone I will over and then she started to hears whisper and he said what do you hear but she didn't paid attention to him but proceed to go upstairs and when toward the attic and when open the door and step inside and then when she was inside it somehow the attic door shut tight and now Kelly was trapped and still had her cell and was still on phone with Joe and what going on?

But Joe said get an reply from her and now he was getting worry about Kelly and now he was about to leave and then Kelly said I am okay and you don't have comes over and I am fine and he said are sure?

Yes I am and I didn't found anything up there so I am going back downstairs and back to my bedroom and I am not scared and I will be okay.

I think that I should come over anyway; no I will get angry if you do but you don't sound like yourself, but I am myself.

About two minute Kelly was near the floor and somehow she slip and fell and Joe heard that and Kelly didn't says anything for few minutes and Joe said well I am coming and Joe locked his apartment and went downstairs and when into the garage and went toward his car and he saw a little girl and she was crying and Joe said what wrong little girl? I am lost and I want to go home.

Where do you live little girl and she said you didn't save me, what?

I don't understand what you are saying and she pointed her finger to the basement and then she said follow me, and he nodded his head and he follow and at this moment woke up said don't go with her.

Kelly got up and shouting on the cell and Joe didn't hear her and now Kelly knew that Joe is in trouble and need to get to him and they are going to hurt him. But he is not listening to me and that little girl is the dark shadow that wants to get Joe. But Kelly knew that she was not alone and it was getting really heavy air in her apartment and the door were open and they were surrounded and then one said you didn't save me, and I am not going to save you neither. But she knew that she had to beat it but she had to be stronger than the entity and she knew that she might lose Joe.

About 3 second she got out and was about to step into the elevator and then before she step inside it was open without an elevator and hold on to the side of and it was really close called for Kelly to died.

Then she decided to take the steps and then the exit door

were not open so she somehow kick it in and the entity follow her inside and was about to push her and so Kelly said I know who you are but don't hurt me but some person heard her saying that and thought I was a crazy but I did see that ghost and I felt the presence and I knew that I had believe it were not hurt me but it did want me.

But I was still in danger so was my friend Joe and now I had to go and save him and at this point I didn't care what might happen.

Kelly got into her red corvette car and storm out of the garage and heading toward to Joe place and time was ticking away and she thought might be too late. But Joe kept following the little girl and she was leaded him into the house and he didn't looked but just kept going and then enter the front door and close it behind him and now Kelly had a premonition about Joe and so she sped and headed to the house on the dark road of Long Island. Then he follow her upstairs toward the library and then the door open up and then girl enter and then he walks inside and it shut the door and sat at the table and then they would holding hands and then Joe let go and tried to get up and they wouldn't let him go and he struggle and somehow he got loose and got up and went toward the door and then it were not open and he banged and turn the doorknob and it didn't move and he pull but he was still stuck in that room.

Whisper to him and said save me before it is too, Kelly hope that you are hearing my voice and then Kelly said don't worry I will get you out of there and I promise.

#  GHOST WORLD

Joe said am in the living world and everything does not seem to be the same has before, I do sees them and now about two minutes ago the sirens when off and the ashes into the air and I think there is no saving me, I have gone to the ghost world and there is no way of coming back, is there?

Joe looked around I am one of them and I cannot stop Kelly coming here but that the risk that she taking to save me but I cannot warns her.

I don't know if I did what were happen to me and I step on the other side and now I will be an earthbound spirit.

But it is not bad but I have no choice this path but it choice I and Kelly didn't come on time and I need to follow the rest of them and now this is my home, so let Kelly comes, I will call her on her cell phone.

I don't know if she going to answer but she will know it me and about ten minute later Joe called Kelly and Kelly answer it and it was a whisper and then a lot of static and she answer and said I will be there soon and don't worry you will be okay.

It was a mist in the "ghost world" and Joe step inside and saw his friend and he said Jeff, nice to sees you again.

Same here come on here sit at the head of the table because you are a new guest and so Joe sat down and then the room was filled and he saw Dana and I cannot believe this, your all here? Yes we are and so are you and one more will be here soon, so you talking about Kelly? Yes of course who else?

120

I don't know but now you belong to the community of ghosts, so you will belong, so one more things that you have to do are get Kelly here.

No, you cannot refuse the man with the big beard and red hair, he will punish you and I will listen, you must, and the mist was getting thicken and thicken and then Kelly knock at the door and no one answer and she walks inside and felt the present of Joe and said I don't sees you but I do feel you.

Don't listen to them they are trying to trick you that you are dead, and you are not and Joe said to Jeff is she telling the truth? Well you have step inside and so yes you are dead, and Kelly don't listen to him, get out of the mist and come back too me. No I when beyond and you cannot save me so just go and don't look back and so Kelly kept on walking away and then stop you can be stronger than he is, he is too powerful for me so I will just go with him.

Kelly said stop comes with me and I will get you out this house and how are you will be able to take me out with this powerful ghost and you will be also trapped in that house too, no I will not and I will fight it do you gets what I am saying to you, yes loud and clear, so I hear you but I don't sees you, and in the room near the library and it is pitch black and I don't sees you, I am in there look closely, I am then she got pushed inside and then the door got lock and she was unable to open it and Joe was not found in the room, you have trick me and I don't like this and I don't belong here, do you hear what I am saying too you. I am hearing what you are saying but it won't let you go and it will not let us go and I don't want be in this situation but I am and I am not blaming you, you should have listen to what I said, sorry but it is too late and this our fate, not mine said Kelly to Joe and said I am going and so this entity is not letting me go but it has a force and then Kelly said don't you smell coffee no I don't but I do and it is very close, so you seeing the ghosts? I think I see them all and then Kelly said I see DANA, do and she is calling me but I am not going to her, one of the entities is just playing trick and wants us to stay.

That what Dana taught me but didn't get her own advice and now she is trapped here and I want to release her, if I have to sacrifice my own life.

Well she is your best friend yes she is, and I am going to help her and I am going help all of us, I do hear what you are saying but I don't know if it going to work. Stop being so negative and it feed on it and don't know it and I don't know but I want to get the hell out now, when I count to ten we should be out of the front door, you got it, yes I do..

Kelly was about to step out but was shove into the corner and then got slapped on her face and shove down to the basement and Dana watched and didn't even wink and Kelly said don't remember me and not a word.

Then Kelly slip and fell down and was out cold and didn't sees anything and they surrounded her and was still didn't move.

Time was ticking and then Joe was just standing still and then was also pushed down next to Kelly but when Joe landed on her body and she didn't move and then Josh said well they are like us. Yes they are.

About one hour later Kelly and Joe would together and said why we are here?

Well you came on the night of the Friday 13th and things just happen.

# NIGHT FRIDAY 13ᵗʰ

 You bought me to the night of the Friday 13th and you didn't know the story what happen in this house and then you knew what happen to Josh and you thought it was just a tale and now it is not and we are ghost.

You knew and yes I knew but I came to save my friends but somehow the house took over and I just got into a daze and confuse and you got me over and that was the plan, do what? To trapped me too, no to help me but it backfire and so I thought it was an make up story and I thought if I told you, you were be superstition but I am not but now I don't feel nothing but just old air.

Watched it don't sees it is repeating the night of the five murder and the killer, and don't you sees it and Joe said yes also the killer got kill by the house and roamed the halls in the house and I know that where is your EVP well I drop it and so it were not work because we are ghosts too, thanks for reminder me.

Looked them all sat at the table and then the killer butcher them into pieces and they are gone and I sass that, and it is repeating it over and over.

The lights are once again on and off and then the windows are closing and opening and I don't like it, so we cannot do anything but we just saw what happen here, and now we are crowded and I don't like it and I am suffocate, so let get out of this room and go where? I don't so do I have think, I guess so.

The clock strike midnight and everything stop and Joe said maybe we have a chance yet to escape, seem like you could be right and I can distract and then you can just step out and I will be behind you. That could be a plan.

So let try and stop chatting and just move quickly out of the door and so okay and then Joe said the door is open and be quiet they will hear you.

Kelly and Joe walks out and looks around and seem like it was clear and walks toward the car and then somehow they were back in the house and so what did happen. I don't know but we are in the house and it does not want to let us go.

Can you tells me what going on and I don't know but I thought we walks out and how did we manage to be in the house,, sure we didn't leave but we did and we walk up to the tree and then about ten second later we were in the house, but don't be angry at me but I am just puzzled so am I so let try again and to leave I think we are stuck here stop saying that's but that is the true.

So Joe walk toward to the door and it was wide open and he went out and walks and went toward the car and was about to go inside and then once again he was standing with them alls and then said I need to speak that I am stuck here and I don't want to be here.

Kelly said well, well we are here and we cannot go home so just listen what I am screw here and I want to see my family and I don't want live in the wood and I want be with my son and my family and I don't want to be a spook and Casper the friendly ghost and so I don't know and he walks though the wall and said I never did that before and I am really an ghost?

Kelly unbelievable and I don't understand how it happen and so how did I get killed? Now Kelly was thinking and didn't remember how it happens. Then she realize it was Friday the 13th and so why did we go there on that date and why did I follow you, I was stupid to follow you and I should have with my instinct but now I am screw because you, thanks a lot for bringing me with you, so now you angry when you twist my arms to go with me, so what wrong with you Kelly, are you confuse or on something, you must be delusion, no I am not look they are staring at us, one of them want to bite off your hand.

Then something just came out and Kelly wanted to scream but she knew she couldn't but just stood still and watched them coming through the walls and then Joe, you can do it too, don't you know that's no and I am not going to do so and well your not going home and so stop saying that.

Listen don't you remember little bit what happen last night, no don't reminder me and I just want to go home, so how many time do I have tell you.

Then the thunder and lighting and it got pitch black and then Kelly walks toward the window and tried to open the window and it was nailed in and then Kelly said they are keeping us inside and we are not allow to go outside and so now your getting it, yes but I don't like it and then Kelly said there are many shadows in this house and not only our, yes it started 10 year ago on Friday the 13th yes I know and but then a family move in and they just vanished in thin air, and never been since yes but we sees them okay.

So they became ghosts and the house just took them yes and it will take more and Kelly said I am going stop this, no it just repeating history, I know that.

Don't want to hear no more just go and leave me alone so fine I will.

Meanwhile Kelly didn't know what was going on and thought it was just a prank but reality didn't hit yet.

# FLESH

Kelly when into a bedroom and got into the bed and fell asleep and woke up the next morning and she looked around and the black flies were buzzing around and she said I need to get rid of those flies and then she looked out of her bedroom and she saw a man with black leather jean and jacket and she was about to called him out and then she looked and he was gone and about ten minute later, he drove up to the front door and Kelly banged at the window and said go away and but he didn't hears her and he step inside and took off his helmet and went into the kitchen to have a glass of water and once again she tried to push him out and then he just stood and looked around and then his buddy came and they alls when inside and they bought beer and whiskey and the music and It loud and then the ghosts started one by one to get rid of and Kelly said go, and no one heard her and now she had to become flesh. One of the biker said what are you doing here sister, and she said I am not your sister and you should leave and he said we are not going leave, we are not afraid of anything, but you should be .do you believe in ghost?

No there is no ghost, little sister and I am your and then a second later she was gone and the biker said I need to found her, and the other biker said why not she is hot and go for it and have some fun and he went toward the stairs and on the bottom and then he was surrounded and he yelled out you guy I am not alone and then they ran in and said hey you pull a good practical joke and he said no I am not it they are not real but ghost well you got high and you don't know what you are saying, I do and let go out of this place now, well no I am staying and have a party, well I am not, you are chicken, no I am not

Are you for real, why do you asked well you just don't sound like we are.

So what era are you from, I don't understand what you are saying I am from this year era no you are not, you are like old fashion clothes, well those were the only clothes that I could found, Joe said to Kelly don't see it, who she is no, she is famous, no you must be kidding, so doesn't act like us and she acted like high class, well maybe she is, and well with a silver spoon and end up here I don't think so she came like we did and didn't go back, well you might be right.

Then she got closer to her and she shook her hand and said well nice too meet you and then just walk away and Kelly said where did she go, I don't I am not going follow her do you understand? Yes totally I do and then Kelly walks out of that room and looked around and sat on couch and did her nail and Joe just search for that lady with a red dress and red bow in her hair but he couldn't find her and just when back to Kelly and then sat down and put the TV and change channel and talked a lot, do you think that we will sees that lady in red again, I bet we will and she smiled and was quiet.

The lady in red is flesh and she is ghost and she goes to her job and I don't believe it but she does and how can we go home maybe we can try to be flesh and then what? Drive home and then do our work. Yes and is that the plan to get back to our place and what peoples will see us, yes, yes I don't know but do want to be stuck in that house? No so let sees what the lady in red does and then we can do it, okay but Dana just came through and said that is wrong, what do you mean. Well you suppose to stay in the house; if we don't so what going happened nothing. Why didn't you leave well now this is my home and world, don't you want to go outside of this home? Sure I do but it will really not change Kelly, so you are not going to listening to me.

No I am not, that is not right but so what. Kelly walk away and then Dana try to convince to stayed but Kelly was listen to the lady in red and that is the bad influence and don't you get it you guy you will not be the same when you turned into flesh you will be evil, no I will not.

Don't listens to what she saying, I won't but you are following her and I don't like it so you don't have, don't turned into flesh and it will be no return. Stop it

Joe when up to her and stand right next to her and the lady in red was gone of the house and Joe said I save you from hell so we are in hell and we are stuck in limbo, better than flesh and hurting other persons among the living.

This is torture and I blame you, Joe you bought me to this house and I thought it was harmless but it was not, and now we live here permanent and I hate is so bad and we cannot go to the door and open it. And walks out of here, so blame me I know it my fault, I hate to apology time after time, stop whining, you make me sick.

Thank a lot so we have to get along so now you mad at me and I don't like being mad but you just make a mistake taking me there, and the lady in red once again appear and comes with me, and she nodded her head and said no I am staying fine and you will not be able to walk out and have a job.

You are saying that you still get a pay check and then you comes back here why you don't go home, I do into this house. And I invite more to come here and then the family grew.

Where do you go and I would like to company you so just come with me, fine I will do it, don't listen and you will sees the world like before and no one will recognize you so they will think nothing about it, that sound AWESOME!

ONCE AGAIN, Joe warn her stop and think what you are

doing, I am I will go with the lady in red and so I can check out my friends if they are okay.

What other reason would I go and then Joe said I will do the same so now not stopping me, no I am not and I am coming too, great, and then Kelly asked the lady in red what is your name? Rose. That is a nice name and so where did comes from south, and Kelly said well I am from the north.

Well you can says I am southern belle, oh Rose well did comes from wealth, well I will not tell you but looks at the clothes I am wearing, not too bad but bit old fashion, so don't critics me, I won't I will not show how to change into flesh, sorry about being rude, so I forgive me this time.

Joe ran up to Rose and said hope that you are not tricking us, I don't understand what you saying and then Rose left alone and what have you done, Joe? Nothing yes you did and I am mad at you and seem like you trust everyone, I do and I think that she was screaming you, what do think I am dumb.

No but you just don't pay attention to me, why should I, now your such a pain in the butt, thank for hang out with me well I have no choice right now but do I have repeat myself to you, no and Joe left and Kelly stood and when the front door open she step out and called out to Rose, and said wait for and then they when inside the car and Rose drove end of road and then stop and said looked around and Kelly said it like old times said Kelly yes and now we have go on and no looking back, okay I won't. EVERYONE WILL THINK THAT YOUR ALIVE, that is awesome, I like it, thanks Rose. No problem at all but we need to come to the house, okay I will help you out. I really had to go back home too sees everyone so I did and then Rose said the rules are to bring them back with you, no I am going to that's do understand what I am saying. So I guess you will not last long has flesh I will send you back to the house, because you don't cooperation with me so go back, do really need to do, don't question me?

Jean Marie Rusin

You were nice at first but you are rude and mean, well you don't listen to the rules and I don't want you with me so, and then suddenly Kelly notice that once again she was not flesh and she was back at the house and then Joe said she was tricking to be just like her, I know Joe and don't reminder about her.

# OPEN HOUSE PART 2

Rose walks inside the house and then she said "I am backing home" and Kelly stayed away from her, and then Kelly notice that the house is for sales.

But two character came Larry and Lenny, to check out the house, they heard story about the haunting and about the murders and the missing persons, so they brought there EVP and digital camera and started to take picture and Lenny when to the basement and Larry was doing the investigate in the library and then door open and Larry step inside and saw them sitting at the table and he said I do not want disturb you, and they didn't says anything to him and then the door shut and one of them pointed to him to sit down and so Larry sat down and hold him and then Larry didn't think they were ghosts but then Lenny called out to him and said let go now I have enough evidence about the haunting, but they were not let go and he pull his hand away and tried to get out and then Larry when upstairs to found Lenny but he didn't know that he went inside the library and Larry looked around and said come on we have to leave but nothing, so Larry decided to go into the library and he was about to open the door and Lenny screen out and said go and run for your life now. No I cannot leave you here, just listen to what I am saying, they won't me go.

Who are they? The ghosts that live in this house and watched out for the lady in red she will tricked and then you will be staying here and then Larry's said is she attractive. Yes she is but she is a ghost, so does she have a hot body? Just go Larry, no you are coming with me do you understand your sister will killed me if I leave you, but don't comes this room, I have warns you. But he still tried to pried open the door but it were not nudge at all.

Two hours later Larry was still standing in the hall and calling out to Lenny to comes out and stop playing his childish game and Lenny said no I am not playing around so leave, and then the storm came in and the lighting stuck the house and then Larry started to sees dark shadows coming toward him but Lenny somehow he ran out and he was still alive and Larry said I was like giving up on you and they approach the door and Rose came up to Larry and put like a spell on him and she started to kiss him and Lenny said go the door open but he was like daze and confuse and she was about too push him to the basement and then Dana step in and said let them go and she somehow pushed her into the wall and vanished and then Larry and Lenny didn't says anything but dash to the door and ran out and when into there cars and Larry said I left my equipment, so what it is the evidence of the haunting and it is expensive, you are nut to step back into the house. But I am going back in.

Sure you waiting for the tragedy too happen to you. no but I know I will be right back, I am going to leave this property and not coming back and you are on your own, thanks a lot buddy and I thought we were a team we are but not in this case, so you sound like you " chicken shit" thanks a lot.

Lenny drove off and then he remember that he left something in the library and so he came back to the house and Larry was still inside and so he called Larry but he didn't answers him, at that point Lenny was started to get mad and furious about being in the house.

So once again Lenny ends up in the library and no one was around and was just about to take his EVP and his camera and then the chandelier fell on Lenny and crush him, and Larry saw him and him almost...

Almost fell to the ground then Rose pick up and gave him

kissed and he was all over her and Kelly step in and said run out of here now it is too late for your friend Lenny but it is not too late for you. He looked at her strangely and torn out and Kelly and Rose started to fight and then Jeff came said girl, girl grow up your not in the living world but then Rose said well I can go out in the world and I want that man? So then Kelly said let Larry go, no he is the love of my life and when I kissed him, I felt it, you don't feel anything you are dead.

Then Kelly open the door and Larry step out and when into his SUV and drove away and you are trouble missy, I am not scare of you, I am just like you. Yes I know but I will get that man back, he will not comes back he know what you are, you better not to inference with me again, you will have a problem. So don't threaten me you cannot do not harm too me. No you don't think so, yes I can and you better watched your back, meanwhile Larry was driving back home with a lot tears in his eyes and couldn't believe his friend was gone.

Then he approach the stop and he saw a lady driving an coverette and heard the horn and then saw her face and now Larry was terrify and sped out of that road and headed to home and it was heavy rain and he couldn't sees anything and he stop at the side of the road and then the lady in red came up to him and pulled him out of the car and said do you know who I am? Larry smiled and said I have to go now and she said wait, I will not hurt you, and he said I don't make love to a ghost, I am human just like you, no you are dead and you are a ghost.

Well don't blow me away I need to be near you and you so hot. But you are not my type but she said a moment ago you were kissing my tender lips.

You were just tricking me to stay in that house and then you were found more peoples and no escape from you so what bought you in the first place to this house, well I don't speak to the dead but you did speak to me.

It doesn't have to change but you killed my friend and now

you want me to be there, no way I am going and the car were not start and what wrong why are you trying to stop me I don't want you, leave me alone.

But Rose was near him and was not let go and somehow Kelly came along said to Rose leave this man alone, and she said no I want him but he doesn't want you. Then Jeff and then Josh said it cannot go on like this.

But Rose said go on and the car started up and they came into the house and they went through the walls and but the man with the red beard and long red hair when after Larry and when Larry started riding toward the cliff, the man with the red beard appear and Larry lose control and skidding down the hill and Larry felt like he had no brake on and then his car hit the tree and he was out cold and about three hours later the ambulance arrive and they took him out of the car and he was barely alive and they also did CPR.

When he was taken to the ambulance it was touch and go but Larry was fighting for his life and the man with the long red beard and was about six feet tall and EMT said we can be losing him but he is fighting inside and he doesn't want to die. Later that they arrive to the hospital and they work on him and then was in ICU with all machine hook up and then he somehow remember what happen to Lenny then he started to wake up and the man with red beard was gone and the nurses said well, he is back and so we will watched him.

Then he looked at the nurse and try to speak and she looked like "Rose" and she unplug the vitalization and then he was not breathing, and the alarm when off and they put him back on time they thought they were lose him.

About ten hours later Larry got up and the nurse said you cannot leave and she told him what happen to him and she mention that she will go there with her fiancé to sees the beautiful house and he tried to warn her but she refuse to listen to him, but Larry was not breathing on his own but he nodded his head but no one looked and but they were too busy with the other patience and then Rose came back and unplug and turned it off and the alarm didn't go off but somehow he didn't died and she was mad and angry and then Liza came in the room said who un plug you and he tried to explains Rose the nurse and Liza called out to Rose and said no don't called her, no I will not call her do you hear me, yes I do but I am not going paid attention to you, why not?

# MOVING IN NEW FAMILY PART 2

Ellie and James moving day and Ellie is pregnant and James is exciting that they will have room for the twin that will be born in about one week from today from today and Ellie fell in love with the house immediately and James was going to have his office at the house and spend time with Ellie and the twin but James walks inside the house and he felt a chill and he just didn't like that unsettle feeling but he kept quiet about what he was feeling and had a bad feeling but meanwhile Ellie said I will open up the library and then get new books and the old books might have some value and James just wanted open up his dentist office but Ellie said it must be in the west wing and so James agree and said it will be separate and so she was happy about that.

But Ellie said you need to set up the crib and get ready for the babies and James said not tonight because I am too exhaust and Ellie when to the master bedroom and when on the bed and place her head on the pillow and meanwhile James looked around and when to the basement and something caught his eye and had to find out what was behind the wall and so he took a shovel and started to banged and banged and the Ellie heard it and got up from the bed and walk down the spiral steps and then toward the basement and open the door and then called out his name " James" what are you doing? Would please stop it and I am trying to sleep and then James said I will stop and then he felt a breeze and a bit of chill go through his body and then he put the shovel next to the walls and when upstairs and close the basement and

136

then he when to the bedroom and Ellie was fast asleep and he when inside the cover and fell the sleep and woke up about 3 am, and heard footstep and got and looked around and about two hour later, Ellie when into labor and she called out to James and said it is time to take me to the hospital and he ran upstairs and then he started to walks down and Ellie said I can walk my babies will get born in the house and James said I will called 911 and the ambulance will comes and Ellie said the babies won't wait so you need to delivery the babies, I cannot do it you must they are coming, and Josh and Jeff said babies are going be born here.

Yes and they will be living with us and he nodded his head and said let go now.

We must tell the others that babies will live here, yes but don't tell everyone I won't. don't tell Rose she will steal the babies for herself and then Rose heard that, I thought that I heard that someone will have babies and I need to sees them, and Jeff and Josh tried to keep her away but she was powerful and so she somehow manage to go outside and turned into flesh and then rang the doorbell and James and answer the door and said welcome to the neighbor and so right now I am busy and Rose said can I help you, are a nurse and she said yes I am and comes on in and my wife will be having babies soon and I don't know what to do and she said boiling some water and get some sheet and James left the room and Ellie said they are coming and Rose said I know and so I will be helping out, and Rose said to breathe and so Ellie did and then about two hours later Ellie gave birth to John and then the second one was born was Jenifer and then Ellie was holding both babies in her arms and then John couldn't breathe and so James called the ambulance and Ellie said they must comes soon and Rose said I will help the baby John and about five minute later, they both were crying but the ambulance came and took the babies and mom to the hospital and Rose just left and James wanted to thank her but then he headed to the hospital to sees his wife and his children.

When Ellie arrive to the hospital and said where are my babies, and the nurse said the doctor checking them out and then Rose came and said I am your neighbor and how are your children and they are fine.

Thank you for helping me and my husband and Rose said that all right, I am glad that I came over and helped out, I really appreciate your help and then she left and James said she sound like an nice person and I think that I should send her flowers and Ellie said yes you should and about twenty minute later, they bought the babies for the feeding and Ellie said John does not seem the same has Jenifer, honey your exhaust, yes I am and I think that you should go home, no I am staying, are you sure? Yes I want to be near my lovely wife and my children. So James stayed near his wife and children and then he overheard something was going on with John and he ran out the room but his wife was fast asleep and but it was a false alarm and he went back to Ellie and hold her hand and fell asleep and the next morning he woke up and asked the nurse where is my wife and she said at the nursery and he got up and walks over and stand by her and then they put Ellie in the wheel chair and bought back into the room and then James said I need to go back to the house to get your stuff that you packed and I will not be long and in the hallway Rose stood and said do you want me to drive you home, and he said I have my car and then walk to the garage and so Rose follow him and then she called out and said wait, my car woke started up were take me home, at that moment James was not sure but he did take her and but somehow flies were buzzes in the car and I don't about this infestation with flies and Rose said I don't know but take me, fine and then they stop at the light and at that moment she looked different and he thought is eyes were playing tricks and then skid on the road and then about half hour later he was home and he drop her off at the house and he when inside and turned off the lights but he notices shadows but then he got back into the car and Rose was standing on the edge of the road and he stop and said why are you home, Rose? Well I just wanted to take a walk and so I just stop for a moment, fine. Then James left her on the end of the road and speed to the hospital and almost collide with a car but didn't hit it.

The other driver yelled and scream said are you crazy? No but my wife just had twin and he nodded and said why are driving so fast, to sees my wife so you could end dead with your driving.

Ben said I live two road ago from you and you live in that haunting house and James said what did you says, you heard me, you said haunting, yes I did.

So I have go now so nice too meet you and drove off and headed and almost didn't stop at the stop sign but then he saw the police car and he slow down a block from the hospital and then park the car into the garage and took the elevator to the fifth floor and when he got to the fifth floor his wife was out of control and said someone took, John and they cannot find him.

James you need to called the police and must find John and I am worry and he is very weak and I don't who took him and meanwhile Rose was rocker the baby in her arms and Jeff said you need to take the baby back to the hospital and it is my baby, listen to me this baby is not your and take it back, no I am keeping it and you cannot take it from me and about Ellie she has Jennifer and so I have John, I will not allow it and you have no right to tell me Jeff and then Josh said what a cute baby, it is my baby and Josh said no it is Ellie baby, you have stolen the innocence child the new born how could?

Fine I will take it back and this baby will be mine when they return to the house, yes and now James had to deal that there new born was missing and then about half hour later the nurse Betty said we found the baby in the crib and Ellie said what kind of hospital lose a child and then they find it in the crib.

I don't like this hospital and they don't know what they are doing and I do want to get discharge and then something when wrong with Ellie and the doctor it is only stress and we need to calm her down and then Rose walk in and said what happen and I don't know exactly what to tell you but the baby was missing for awhile oh I sees so did they misplace the baby, yes and Ellie is fragile and a little paranoid right so I will let her to rest and so can we go for coffee and James said of course seem like went I need a friend, you are around so tell me about you well I was an in fashion but now I am working into radio and so that sound exciting, yes it is so have a seat and what kind of coffee do like well hazelnut and with cream and Rose said well I will have a French vanilla no cream and so what do you do James well I am an dentist and your teeth are so white, thank so, you will be going to the city? No I will be having a office in the house so that great and then Rose said I will make a appointment with you but your teeth are so prefect, I do care for my teeth and then Rose got up in hurried and said I have to go and she said I will talk with you later and nice meeting you and so I have go the appointment and Rose left and Ben stop by and you are the lunatic driver, thanks, and so what are here to lecture me? No I am not and then James said I have go back to wife and son and daughter new born and Ben said hope that you really don't live in that house, so what wrong with that house, when you have time to talked I will give the history of the house and then meanwhile Rose was looking went Ben was talking to him and Rose didn't like Ben and so she knew that she had run into Ben, because she didn't want the secrets of the house too comes out and James went to visit his wife and his twin and somehow Rose manage to run into Ben and accidental and said hi, and he said wow you are hot, and she smiled and said thanks and do you want to walk with me and he said my pleasure. Rose smiled said thank you being so kind, I want you Rose, oh you do well if you catch me you will have me, is that an promise, maybe I but I doubt that you will get me James I believe that Ben is the one that I want. No you must be kidding? No I am not looks at my face so what does it mean, just leave me alone fine and James storm out and was calling out Ben and he wanted to fight with him. Went Ben step out to fight with James and James said I am going to fight with you and Ben punch him out and he was on the ground and the James got up and hit his face and Ben fell and almost hit the cement on the ground and so he was lucky but those faces were looking out of the house and said I guess we will have more to be guest and residence oh I sees. So do think that Rose will get them both? Yes I do and she knows how so she is one clever ghost. James came up to Ben and said leave us alone and Ellie said well I don't know what going on in this house but I don't want to stayed but James said this house is what we were looking and Ellie said we have too many things going on in this house and I don't want my babies to come back here when they get born, I put all over saving here and now you don't like it here and then Rose came out and said missy I am going have one of your baby and Ellie said you are not. I am going to take the child from you and you will only one child and Ellie said no I will have both children and Rose said wait until your babies will be born and Ellie was argument with Rose and then she was gone and then Ellie started to have tears in her eyes and then said no one will steal my babies and James said don't get stress and everything will be okay and you can trust me.

# TWINS ARE BORN

Night of the birth of the boys, and it occurs around 315 am and Ellie cried out and said James it is time to go to the hospital and James was not getting up and the water broke and still James was still in bed and now Ellie tried to open the bedroom door and it would not move and then she shook James and he was in a deep sleep and then Rose appear and said this child will be mine the first born in this house and no you cannot take my baby and then Ellie fell to the floor with an big stump and then James got up and said honey are you okay and he notice the water broke and he said I get you to the hospital and then Rose said no you are not leaving and then the rest of them enter and the man with the red beard pull him out the room and James was banged on the door and somehow Josh came and said I will helped you too get back into the room and I will open the door and you will be able to leave and you will not be stuck in this house like we are so, so hurried before Rose take your child and killed it and make it like one of us, stop her and the only way is by love and Rose is powerless by that, thanks for telling do it and just don't stand go inside and get your wife and babies and run has fast you can but I cannot run with my wife Ellie the babies are coming just get out I have warns you. Ellie sat on the couch and the labor started and James and said I sees one of the baby head so push and so Ellie did and Rose looking behind the couch and said it is an boy and about one hour later the second son was born and Ellie said first born will be called Oliver and then the second son will be called Owen and then

142

Rose said looks at Owen he looks different from Oliver and James said don't listen to her both babies are the same and then Ellie said looks Owen is different and then Rose grab Owen and said this is my baby and Ellie scream and said don't take my baby from me, and Rose just vanished and Owen was gone and Ellie was crying and s screaming and the ambulance came and said we came to take your wife and son to the hospital and Ellie was in a bad ways and said I had two sons and one is missing and James said no she is delusion and trying to protection Oliver from Rose and Ellie started to yelled and scream I want my son back and James whisperers quiet and said Rose will hear you and go with Oliver and I will meet at the hospital and so Ellie when inside the ambulance and got the hospital and about half hour later James came to her room and said I will get Owen back for you and me, I promise. You believe me, of course I was in the room when Rose stole Owen and I search the house and I will bring the Owen too you the hospital, I promise you and I love you so much giving me two sons and Ellie calm down and they bought Oliver and he was crying and then he stop and the nurse took the baby to the nursery and Eliie said I don't want to leave my baby alone and about half hour later Rose came into the hospital room and said to Ellie, I took the wrong baby and now I will take Oliver and Ellie said where is Owen and Rose didn't says a word and left and then James came in and said was Rose here? No she cannot take Owen but she did and now we have Oliver and but Oliver is not crying something wrong with him and I don't know but what have Rose too our babies? Rose can answers that but I cannot, but why ours babies, it is the house and we shouldn't have move in because the curse, you mean it is an haunted house and there are ghosts and I know that's and but what drove us to buy it and I don't but it is too late, we will find Oliver and we will have both babies, yes we will. NO I will not allow her to have my son, how are you going to stop her and I don't but I will and when she is flesh and I will follow her where ever she goes and I will get my son back and she looks at Oliver and he has an mark on his nose and his face is not the same has I remember what did she do our baby and then Oliver cried and Ellie pick him up and I think that Oliver saw Owen and we need to find him and take them both out of this house and James do you understand what I am saying and I do and don't get her angry and then we might not find Owen and Ellie said don't worry about it we will, you don't know who you are dealing with and I am not scare of Rose and I will be stronger with my love and I will get my child back and how do you know that you will and I feel him and he is very close to me and I want him back and James said sure I want my son back too and so let search for him but first we need to get Oliver out of the house to my mom house and he will be safe and then Ellie felt an chill and said I felt some presence and I don't know if it was Rose and we have a lot of ghosts in this house and they can be helping her and I don't like it.

Listen Ellie and I think that Rose heard you in the room and I think she is guard Owen and so she will not let him go and you will be harm by her if he tried to get your son back and Ellie said our son, so don't correct me but seem like you are afraid of her and I am not and I am going to get him back.

Just watched your back and your step when you deal with Rose and I will so can you take Oliver to my mom and I will looked around and maybe I will spotted him and when Rose leave the house and so okay I am going and make sure that you pack his stuff and then you will not have comes back what you forgot, I got everything and he had Oliver in his hands and then he was trying to open the door and but it were open and then he smell the perfume of Rose and said let me go and my son and then it felt like an wind and it open and he walks out and went to the car and Ellie said called me when you get there and she shut the door and yelled out to Rose and said where Owen? You will never get him back and you will not sees his face again what have you done too him?

#  LOST CHILD

One stormy night Ellie was up about 315 am and heard footstep and thought it was James and then suddenly the door with an banged and Ellie got up and when out in the halls and saw something that happen a long time ago and so she was shadows and then she noises outside of her door and then she thought it was Owen. But then she saw that man with the red hair and beard coming toward her and then she was about to scream and then James got up and said what are doing sleepwalking again, and she said I don't want to stayed here anymore and James said why not? Don't you want to find Owen? I do but it is an risk for Oliver and I think that we should send him away, I will not allow that he is staying here but he is in danger and we cannot stayed here and so let go no, said we are leaving and Ellie we surround by ghosts.

They are coming how do you know I see them coming they are don't you see them, then James got pushed down the stairs and then Ellie slip and tumble downstairs and then Oliver crying, then somehow Ellie grab the railing, and pull herself up and went to get Oliver and you are not getting this son, and walk up to his room and locked the door and James called out and Ellie said don't you believe me now? I do and help me out and we will leave and there no reason to looks for Owen and he is gone forever and then somehow Owen and Oliver together and Ellie said did bring him to James and he said I didn't know that he was in the room and then Rose stood said this is the last time that you will sees Owen, don't harm him it my son and Rose said no it mind.

Don't do this to me Rose. You must been a mother before and I sees that you love this child and but one thing that child belong to me and not you and just let him go and I do want to hold my son and then Rose disappear and she was gone and so was Owen and I am begged you, and James said you lose him forever don't says that James and I will get him back and I will show that Rose will not keep my son. Ellie decided to search the whole house and trance of Owen and then James said to Ellie it is time to leave and Ellie refused and when upstairs and locked the door and holding Oliver so tight and somehow James broke down the door and when inside and said get your stuff and we are leaving and Ellie said take Oliver and I will stayed in this house and James said no I am not going without you and said you do love me and my son you leave tonight and so James pack a bag for himself and for Oliver and was going back to Ellie and she refuse to answer him and he banged at the door but then gave up and left the house and put Oliver into the car seat and started up the car and left and Ellie was looking out of the window and then it started with the sounds and voice and a baby crying and Ellie looks and nothing and then started going into the basement where she felt some eerie sound and a chill in the air and meanwhile James drove up to the end of the driveway and thought maybe I should go back but then he sped away and he was far gone and when on to the highway and headed to the highway but at first he couldn't believe that Rose was sitting in back with Owen and he suddenly stop and said you bought my son back and Rose said yes and because I want to be with you and Eliie will never come to you again, what have done to my wife said James?

Well she refuses to leave the house and now she will be one of us, what do mean? Well you don't know, and then she show him what she was and he was afraid and stop the car and almost hit the tree and Oliver looks at Owen, and started to cried and James said what wrong with my sons?

You don't know James they are my babies and not Ellie and

I don't understand and meanwhile Ellie was in the basement and the door were not open and she started calling out and no one came but Josh came and said lady what are you doing here? I thought you left with your husband and children and who are you and I used to live here with my parents, so what happen?

I cannot tell you the man with the red hair and long beard will hurt me if I tell you and I don't understand but do not go into the library. But why not, why don't you do something about it...

Lady I have warn you and I hope that just walk out of this house before 315 am and so what going to happen if I don't go and then he was gone.

Ellie was about to use her cell phone to called James but then she decided to looks around more and then it was about 1 am and so she just wanderer in the house searching for her son and no trance and then sat down on the couch and fell asleep and then she was surrounded and then she suddenly woke up and they were standing right next to her and she said leave my house and they said this is our house and now you are an residence of this house and I am I live her and this is my home and you will not force me out and do you understand what I am saying well this is our home and she said I will called the police for intruders, well we are not intruders and we live here and you cannot chase us away, yes I will and she tried to make an called but no dial tone and she said why did you disconnect the phone we have not.

Now she was getting frighten and scare what was happening and they were coming through the walls and Josh said I told you and you didn't leave you should have left but I think Rose trick you and so now you are trapped.

No I am trapped and I will be able to leave the house.

# GHOSTLY ENCOUNTERS

Ellie looks and didn't know which ways to get out and every time that she tried she was block by the tall red hair beard man and so she said what do you want from me and she was walking with an limp with his leg and stop and pick up the knife and was toward her and somehow he missed her and she ran out of that room and ended up in dark hallway and no candles and no flashlight and but pitch black and so she was confuse and lost and he was like an inch away from her and she started to run to the end of the hall and the doors started to close and she was mix up and when into the blue room and then the door shut and was banged and yelling and said I don't want to be here and then he appear to her and said don't hurt me, but then lighting and thunder and the next morning she was in bed and said was having an bad nightmare? She called out to James and no one answer and then she walk down to the living room but it didn't feel the same and she said it was only a bad dream and then she tried her cell phone to called James and every time that she did it was static and what going on here and then she saw the man with the red beard and was about to throw her down the floor and Josh said she is one of us and leave her alone, and he walks away.

Meanwhile James with the two sons and he left the boys with Rose and said you take care of the babies and I am going to get Ellie back and Rose said the man with the red beard has her and it is too late, no it is not and left and didn't think about boys just about Ellie.

Then she got an Omni feeling with the eerie and sound that she cannot knowledge and think that it is all in her mind but then she approach the door it just open and then close and thought what going on and then saw that dark shadow and coming closer to Ellie and she was about to scream but she couldn't scream like something was holding and couldn't speak and now she was really getting scare and then she heard footstep coming closer and was about to touch her and then felt the chill in the air like an mist and it was gone and then Ellie just stood and said I should have left the house and was about to go back, and started to pack and then black flies and cockroaches were on her hand and the temperature was lower and so she could sees her breathe and now she realize that she was not alone but something was just haunting her and now Ellie was about to walk out of her door and saw that man with the red beard and said you are home and she said no I am not I am going she got near the door walks a little ways to the halls but she couldn't leave and he said and you are not going anywhere and you staying and she saw him and then a moment he was gone and she was about to step out and Josh said Ellie don't see yourself and don't know that you will never leave, and Ellie I am going now and you will not stop me and so let me go to family and Josh said we are your family now and she said no you are not and then she was surrounded by them and so she begged to be let go and they alls you had an chance and you blow it by staying here free will and you were not force and Ellie said I know but I now I do want to go out of here and so let me go! No, we cannot and you must stay and your children are being taking care of. Stop saying that I don't want to hear that and I just wants my children and my husband you will never sees them again and don't hear me? No I just want to leave but you choice to stayed and so that is what is you fate and I don't believe you and she tried to open the door and every time that she tried to walks out she was back inside and now she was scare and true that she like the rest of the residence of the house and then she asked went did this happen to me? You don't remember the night of the fire and what fire? I don't know and I don't remember and so you loss your husband and two sons but they are not here and they are gone yes they when with Rose and she shown them how to become flesh and so you are saying they are alive? No they are not and they are like you and us and I am not like you. So what does that mean? Well you came here and you didn't leave so you stayed and so welcome to the house stop that's and I don't like it here.

Then Ellie started to called out and for James and the boys but they didn't comes back and but she saw those "GHOSTS" and they were coming through the walls and grabbing Ellie and said leave me alone, and called out James I need you and I want you and comes and get me and meanwhile that James and the boys were on the ways with Rose and she was going to show them an special place but they were shock and Owen and Oliver said she is evil take us away from here and she shown them her grave stone and the boys were terrify and the whole thing and then they left and but they were not too far from the house and so Rose said do you comes to come back inside with me? The boys nodded and said no we are not going into that house and James almost step inside but someone push him out and he got back into the car and Rose when inside and just disappear in thin air and now James said I must have doze off and I having an bad dream and so James when to the boys and drove off an mile away and then saw Ellie looking out of the window and so James said to the boys I need to go back inside to get your mom and they said don't go.

But he didn't listen too the boys and they sat for hours and hours and no one didn't comes out of the house so then two boys decided to go inside and then they all were in the house and they looked around with spider webs and black flies hitting the window and Oliver said I don't like this place, it spooky!

# WHITE NOISE

So where is dad? I don't sees him but I do hear footstep and I don't like it here but have been here before don't you remember when we were born and then taken, yes I do. Remember the night when the lights when out but then what happen she was searching for you in the house and I couldn't find her so I just left the house and never came back until I got an premonition and so I wanted to go back and so I took you guys to search and it is 10 year ago and you were infant and now I want to take her home and Owen said you are scaring us and so don't and I don't want to be here, but why because of Rose. No this house give me the creep and let go dad no we are staying you have lost it dad and we are going back to the car now and you can go by yourself, no you are two are going inside this was your home. Your not going make we and we are staying in the car and you are delusion and you will not find her inside so let leave now before dusk and no I will go inside you are going too.

Owen and Oliver refuse to step inside the house and Owen has visions and Oliver hears voices and said no we are not, so James pull Owen out and then Oliver and pull them in and they started to screams and somehow Owen got out and Oliver was stuck inside and Owen said I will get you out if I can.

The lights started to flicker and then the doors would shut tight and James and Oliver were inside the house and it make crackling and Omni feeling and eerie inside and those shadow peoples coming out of the walls. James said this was a mistake that I bought you in the house and Oliver and I warn you but you were stubborn to listen and so it is your fault and now do we leave? I don't know son but I will figure out a plan so maybe Owen can called someone, no one will listen to an 11 year old boy they will think it is an practical joke and so we are doom because you wanted to find her and it was so many years. I know but we need to get out now. Owen will not called anyone they will stop him and he will be lost and we will be gone too and no trance of us and that how you did it dad and now we are not going we are stuck with GHOSTS, and Shadow Peoples they have tricked you and now we are not among the living do hears what I said dad? Yes but I need to find my wife and your mother, you mean Ellie and she is your mom but Rose raise us, she did but she also an ghost are nuts, dad, suddenly it got pitch black and Oliver said that was so an bad idea to comes here, so you were born here and then I took you away because your mom said to keeps you and your brother safe but now you got us in danger and mother will be angry at you for bringing us here.

I think that Owen will escape with no harm and so he can contact grandma and how will he get there? He will not be safe alone, I have the premonition that he will be in danger by a predator and so he could died. What are you saying you make a mistake by coming back to this haunting house? Oliver tell me more I cannot and then Rose appear and said where is Owen, he is my son Oliver is not the one I want, and then she tried pull James through the floor and the floor were bleeding and Oliver somehow ran toward the library and saw the man with the red beard and he just when through him but the red hair man tried to grab him and then Oliver had an chance to get out of the window in the library but he called out for his dad but didn't comes and he just out through the window and was on the roof and Oliver was a bit shaking for an 11 year old boy with the dark completion and black hair that brown eyes and they were like sparkle in his eyes and he called out to Owen and but he didn't hear him but then he saw some railing and climb down and meanwhile James called out said Oliver and said to Rose what have you done to my son? I didn't do anything but he left and that is not good, they house need 2 more and the house will be filled, Rose walks back and forward and then he saw her really face that was old and wrinkle and her hair was gray and so a bit long and she was about 5 feet 8 inch tall and had an nice figure and then the man with the red beard appear and pull him into the basement and he saw Ellie and said you are here? But why have you comes back here? I told to stayed away but you never listen to me, where are my sons? They are not here but you did you bring them here and I told no. but the red hair man stop her talking so that James said to Ellie come with me, and said no I cannot go with you I have to stayed here I don't understand but you will soon and you make our sons into orphans and why did you., and she walks away and she was not there, come back Ellie, I need you and please and the man with red beard push James down and was out cold and the next morning James was one of them.

James woke up and said what happen and the next thing he was walking through walls, don't tell me Ellie I don't remember what happen but you will.

You are with me and hope that our sons are safe and not in an tragedy and I don't them dead like we are and don't worry they are probably far away and they will be orphan and they will be in foster care and think that they will find an place and live there but I don't about foods and shelter and they will died.

So James and Ellie were together once again and so now we will not be alone but you need to follow the rules of the house and we will be fine and why are so scare Ellie because the man with the red beard is evil and he wanted to control us and what to do and not what?

# THE BEGINNING

 Ellie telling James how all the haunting started on Friday 13th and so there were a murder but it was 10 year ago and that house cause murder and suicide in the house every ten year and it will continue when that ghost with the red beard that murder those persons and someone killed him and it is like an urban legend and so that how the house get more victims and so there is no escape, how do you know the history of the house, I just find out recent and not before and if I did I were never came to this house and so that how the tragedy started and it goes on and on and no end.

We cannot step out of the house because the house is keeping us here and so we are ghosts and we cannot leave this house, I know what you saying but we are stuck here.

Also I learned the house was build in an cemetery and so they remove some bodies but some were left underneath and they enter the house and the bad things started to happen. But every night the murders just repeat every night and you sees what happen to the victim and then the killer become the victim and so that how the tales were told and went an child is born and the house started to live again and when you enter the house and you cannot escape and so that is your destiny and you will be in the house forever and that is not good and so like we are? Yes and we just stayed and we cannot warns anyone to leave and so it just grow more and more peoples become Ghosts and they just stayed in the house just like we. Yes and I am glad that our sons escape from here, I hope they did. So are you listening to the history of this house and when did you find out just recent and if I knew I were refuse to step my foot inside and so now we cannot go back home and we are stuck here, and then Rose said if you change into flesh and you will be able to leave and do the ordinary things, well the man with red hair and beard will not let us go so we cannot change into flesh, he will killed us again and we will feel the pain.

So we need to get rid of the man with red hair and beard and so how just make him go into the light and trick him, he is not stupid and he will get revenge on you and then you will be sorry, and it did happen before and they were gone.

Rose is trying to scare us from that man and you are not afraid of him and then Rose said no he is afraid of me, and Ellie said why? Because I was the one that did all the killing in this house and now he know that I can just send him into the light and he will not be here and haunting anyone anymore, you kill me and then you killed James, and the rest of them, yes I did and so I will get more, but I do not understand why and why did you do it and why did you want me and my family that were be complete don't understand that a family should be together and now yours sons are out there and no family to love and care you have ruin my family, the night that my sons were born and you stolen them and then you gave one back somehow I had both and now they are 11 year old a and they don't have a family but they will they are not too far from here and will bring them back, and Josh appear and said don't let her out your boys will be in danger and you somehow you need to walks out and called there names and tell them to run for they lives.

Rose will not let us leave she is not that powerful and you must not fear her and I have learn her ways, so you step out and tell your boys to leave this property now, and Ellie said I will keep her distract and you tell them get away and they will be fine, that right said Josh and then Rose came and said I heard what you said but I see the boys approaching the yard and they heard my voice and they will be home soon, no said Ellie, they will not comes back and then Rose pushed Ellie on the floor and the doors and windows started to open and the boys now looks back and saw many shadows in the window and said let leave and we can make it to the end of road into the town.

Well you told your husband about this house but it too late for both of you. You would not listen and you still would move in but don't listen to yourself, well I am telling the story don't think it is too late so just forget about it.

Then Ellie walks out on James and said why did leave and I didn't says anything and it my entire fault for moving into this haunting house.

So I did fall in love when I step inside and so did you and so we bought the house so it could been my fault more because of Al that real estate told me about this place was cheap and it was not expensive so I thought about it and then I show you and you love it and I didn't know the history, so never mind.

We cannot change what happen here and so we just have to stayed and but in someway we plan to stayed and raise ours children but it just didn't work out that way and I just wander if Owen and Oliver are safe.

So keep on telling me about this house and what kind of tragedy happen here and probably not that bad, come on be serious and you what happen to us and it happen to many more and just pull in more and more and it doesn't stop and it is wrong and I do want to help the next peoples that move into the house that were escape the mayhem in here and were leave and they are not even looking for us because we just vanished in thin air, that is true.

# SHADOW PEOPLES

Yes we vanished in thin air and they are not looking for us and they that we just abandon the house and left and now they will resell the house and new peoples will move in and so we need to warns them from the "Shadow Peoples" and they are some evil bunch and so they will trick them and they will killed them in an instantly and so you know what happen to us but looks out they are lurking out of the walls and they will attack us, no they will not.

Some are white shadows but they dark one are the bad one and I don't know how many there are in this house and they do watch our move.

Then the lights flicker and then doors shut tight and the creaking sound front the basement and so eerie sound and then loud ominous bang and so I know, so how long have been here and then suddenly Josh appear ands said they are coming and so leave this perimeter now.

I don't understand, how long have you been here and don't know the protocol about the shadow peoples they want there space and you are in it.

You have been warned and the last time do you understand? Sure aren't we part of the clan anyway. You are not supposed to speak that way.

I am going to speak and it is my house, please be quiet and we will get punish because of your loud mouth and then he just continue speaking and didn't listen to Josh and one of the dark shadow threw him downstairs and he landed on the cement floor and bang his head.

Then Ellie said well if you were alive you were been dead, thank a lot but what happen well he were out of line and they wanted us out. They are all around us and we have no escape but we are like them all ready so why run? What are you saying Ellie, do sees what I see? No ours boys are coming home to us but I will not allowance it do understand? Yes but if they are left alone they will be orphan and I will not let ours boys to alone without us, James steps in and yelled out and said go ways from here now, run and have an life do you hear me? Owen said yes we do and they just about to go inside but they turned around and dash away quickly and Oliver was out of breathe and said that was close and we need to leave and find our grandma and that a good idea and I hope that the shadows peoples won't follow us. They won't how you know I don't know but be quiet I see something in the road, what is it?

I think it a little girl with a doll and looking strangely at us and I think she want us and she want us to go back we will not go back there again it might pull us but don't let it. Be strong do you hear me and don't look into her eyes.

Owen and Oliver thought they were safe and near the highway and away from that haunting house but they were still in the zone and trap, like the force were not let them go, and Owen and Oliver didn't like what was happenings but Oliver said I have an plan to get ways from here, just wait for what?

Owen said I want to be with Mom and dad don't you no that ways. I don't understand and I sees that dark shadow approaching us and the little girl is gone and I think we have no escape, don't says that" I am scare and frighten of the dark, so am I Oliver, and I think if we are stronger than the dark shadow we will be able to go to grandma house and live with her, I like that ok when I count to ten we run like we never did and so remember I am in back of you and we will be okay, are you sure about that? Don't question me, then they saw Rose and Rose lock the gate and Owen said we need to open it and to leave so will Rose let us go? She was the one that locked the gate and she wants us to stayed, no ways I am letting her keep us. How are you going to stop them and I don't know but I am not going to let them keeps us. We are stuck here and we have no escape so what are you saying about that's I don't want to be here.

Don't Owen don't go inside and you will be trapped forever if you inside mom had warns you and me and so we are leaving this place and don't looks back it will drive you back inside and we will not sees the daylight again, how do you know Oliver, Rose told me and I have listen clearly and so I am going back and you are not neither. Meanwhile James and Ellie were roaming in the house and they were saying it were be nice to sees our boys again!

Ellie stared out of the window and she saw them walking away from the house and she was attempt to called them but James said let them go! Ellie got close to James and said don't let me go! I won't and the man with the red beard came close and torn her away from James and said Ellie will be mine, and James said no she is my wife and lay off and then the man with red beard threw James across the room and James landed on the floor and said don't touch my wife again. Then James heard someone calling out his name and it was Oliver and said we are coming in and someone James block the door and Owen said are you crazy? No but I were like to sees my mom and dad don't you not now, comes on Oliver, you want to stayed in this house and it will take you quickly and how do you know I have been here with Rose and it is eerie and creepy and you don't want to run into that man with the red beard.

# A DARK PLACE

Owen was looking inside the window and then he saw the man with the red beard and he was about to pull Owen inside and Oliver pull him away and said we are not staying, fine and you were right about this place and then rest of the spirit were just lurking out and wanted them to be resident of the house and Owen said to Oliver that we were born here and that why we came back, yes it was that reason but now we have leave this " dark place" and never speak about it again.

Promise not a word to anyone that we came to this haunting house that once we live and the stories that been told about a boy name Josh and he was like seeing the dead and saw the murder that occurs 10 year ago and so we go now. Yes I am ready to say goodbye and not going back, good, I like to far way and not near here again, so tell me more about Josh. Well the story is that the first family that bought the house and didn't know about the murders until Josh was seeing things and things started to happen and so that evil man started the whole things about the haunting and it just grew each time and more were missing and, more bodies were discover but the spirit continue to haunted the house and more victim of the house and no stopping so that why we cannot step in that house again, do you hear me? Yes I do and that why we are leaving and not looking back, so the " dark place and the eerie sound and the Omni feeling, you get when you are in the house and you feel the heaviest in your body and you are unable to move do you get it Oliver. The worst fear is that when

160

you step inside and you are trapped forever and I don't want to be trap.

But we will be alone and without parents and who will raise us? We are going to grandma and she will know what to do and she will teach us and raise us and we will have a good home and you think so? Said Owen, yes I believe so and so we will be fine. So we leave here and we have to walks for mile and mile to get to the main road and then we will get a ride to grandma? Yes and then we will be safe and meanwhile James and Ellie were saying hope the boys are fine and then Rose shown up and said they are far away from here and so they will make it and so you have too not worry and so James and Ellie just when through the walls and into there room and Ellie was calm and relax and so James got close to Ellie and they kiss and said now I will rest and James said I will rest with you if you don't mind and then Rose came in and said James I want to talk with you and Ellie said see what she wants. And James step next to her and said, what do you wants from me? Well do I need a motive? I don't know you, yes you do and you know one of the boys is mine and Ellie doesn't know, and she will never know, do you understand? Yes I do!

James was about to choke her and she said I am all ready dead and you cannot kill me do you understand and then Ellie step out of the room but she didn't go through the wall and Josh came and said the "Dark one" doesn't like you and James and he want to get rid of you and Ellie said how can he? We are all ready dead, he will threw you out of the house and you and James will roam the cemetery and you will be able to come back inside, what? We will be banned? Yes and Rose will tried to get James inside and you will roam alone in the dark, no it will not happen, I have warns you and you just watched yourself, I will and you be careful, thanks! I see the dark shadow coming closer and closer and I think that he will feel me and what will happen, I don't know but I am dead what else I don't know just move away from the dark one he is the evil one, meanwhile Owen and Oliver would walking felt someone was following them oh my god it the dark one is following us and he will grab us, no he will not and we will escape the dark one, and dark place is worst. Don't let it grab you, don't worry about it and I will feel fine and no more, I don't see the dark one and the sun is going up and I think it gone, do you think so, yes.

They walks for miles and miles and a car swerve toward Oliver and Owen push him away, Owen fell down and got hit and ran to him and lifted him and but he was fine….

Then they both walks away and the car just off the cliff, about a minute later, they saw the ghosts, then Owen said you tried to killed me and die, because you wanted to killed me and you were save by Oliver and how I will have go to that house that need more resident and now you are free to go where ever you want to go and now I need to go home..

About a minute later the rain came and thunder and lighting and now Owen and Oliver need to found shelter and so they walks and walks and they reach an store but it was close and they said it looks like it was abandon and with cobweb on and dirty and so Owen said let break in and Oliver said no I don't feel right about that's you are chicken and you don't want to explore the possibly and you are chicken, no I am not stop saying and then the pouring rain came really hard and Owen broke the window and walk inside and said I need to sleep a little and Oliver said I stay awake for now. I will watched out for anyone that approaches us and we will not be trapped and I am a little scare but I am fine and I think we will reach grandma house but now I need to get an snooze and Oliver said well I will looks out and about one hour later they were fast an sleep and so the clock rang at 315 am Oliver woke quickly and said what going on here and I thought you were awake and no one was there but Oliver felt the present and said we are not alone here!

# WE ARE NOT ALONE
# SOMEONE IS HERE

I just feel it and I know it want us and don't be scare and I think we are surrounded by the ghosts in this place and then Oliver heard a whisperer and said I heard an man voice and he said " get out of here" and then someone touch me and it was cold has ice and then I felt the eerie feeling with the Omni sound and I think that we better get out of here now, do you understand, yes and I think we should go now, and they ran out of that place and a car was coming by and it was an old black Cadillac and so it looks like no one was inside and now they both panic and said let get out of here now. And Oliver said let me get my carry on bag and the water and we have about two miles away to grandma house and hope that we will make it soon without any distract, I agree, and once again, Owen was a bit busy and he just snuck inside and Oliver was walking on the sidewalk and then called out Owen, where are you? Then he looks back at the store and walks back and grab Owen and said no more pit stop and just get to grandma house and we will be safe and then Owen said look we are back where we started and we are back at the house how can it be? I don't know but I don't like it and so we better walks and get out of this place and they walks about a mile more and they ended up at the store inside and they were locked up and said we didn't go inside so how did we get here? I believe that they don't want us to leave and it is our destiny and so we belong here, no we don't and stop saying that's, I refuse to listen to your nonsense and I think we just have break the curse and it will let us go! I don't understand what you are saying and I don't want to be an resident at the house neither so let started walks more miles they got and once they reach the end of the road somehow they ended up in that store, what are doing here again said Oliver to Owen, it just want us, this place feel familiar and I think we are in one of the room in the house but we didn't enter the house, did we? I don't remember but move forward and we will get out here, and then a dark shadow appear and they said no we are in trouble and we are in the house, why did we enter? Did we enter? I don't think this place is tricking us to think that we are in the house and just step out and don't looks back and we will be fine and then " Josh" appear and said what wrong with you guys? Why are you leaving and why did you step in the house when I warns you and your parents and then Rose appear and said my boys are home, and Owen said your not my mom and so leave us alone and then James and Ellie came and said step out and close the door behind you and Rose locked the door and they couldn't open it and then Josh said pull Rose away and the door open and they ran out and didn't looks back and they saw the yard was an cemetery and so we are safe now, said Owen and Oliver and now we can go to safe place and before they left Ellie came and gave them a hug and kiss and James stood next to them and shook there hand and said some day we will sees each others.

But go now and said tomorrow will be Friday 13th and it will happen again so about every ten years and it will occurs again, and they started to cried and Ellie said to the boys don't forget us and never comes back here again, do you hear me? Yes we do and so just get out of here now and go. But Owen was trying to say that he wants to stay and Ellie said you belonged here and go with your brother now, okay mom.

Now they close the door behind them the wind got stronger and stronger and it was the tree branches were falling and it almost hit Owen but miss by an inch and then Oliver said I never knew there was an lakes near by and Oliver don't think about going swimming, no I am not but it nice and I just want to look at it, but don't go near the edge and so I won't and they looks but the storm was getting stronger and stronger and they found an barn in the wood and they stayed until the storm was over and they kept on walking and walking and they reach the highway and now they were crossing the bridge and they were in New York City and they were in Manhattan and they were relief and they had to found there grandma but they knew that she live in the " Drake" and they didn't know what floor and they enter and the guard asked what are doing here, we are looking for our grandma and so what her name Lilac and so what floor is she? Well boys she doesn't live here anymore so do have a forward address, sorry we don't, now what Owen? I don't know but we need to find her now, and about a minute later, Oliver said I saw Grandma and she does live here and he lies to us and she live on the 12th floor, so let take the elevator to that floor and knock at each door, we will get into trouble so what!

About one hour later, they were on the 12th floor and they started to knocked at each door and then an silver lady with blue eyes and about 5ft 3 inch tall and said I think that I know you and then said come in you must be my grandchildren and they step inside the apartment and it was a bit dark and creepy and eerie sound and Oliver whisperer to Owen said let get out of here, we just got here, well I just like the feeling about this place and then he said it is not grandma, are you paranoid? No looks around and it has cobweb and it is dirty and she has some old dress don't you sees it? Okay your right, I do sees it and then they looks at her face and it pale and her hands are wrinkle and cold and they felt the chill and Owen said tried to open the door and it were not open and the guard came up and said what are you doing here? I told you she not here, well then the old lady grab the guard and he was gone and now Owen and Oliver ran out and push the elevator button and down they step inside and when down and didn't looks back and said we need to find grandma now.

But they search and search and they had no trace of located her, and how what? We need to find a place to sleep and eat and get a shower. Yes I know but we are being follow and we are not alone the "dark shadow are following us and it is not good and well it might be an reason, yes because some how we are connect to the house because we were born there, yes and that our legacy and what? I don't want to go back there, I don't want neither and about ten minute later they were at Broadway and then near time square and they saw many shadows that they were lurking and trying to touch them and then Owen said looks at that place and I think that grandma lives here, and they push the door bell and old person answer and said you must be Owen and Oliver and I been waited for you to comes, I got an called from your mom and said you too were on your ways and but they didn't says about what happen in the house and they kept to themselves about the activities and but very quiet but Grandma knew that they were keeping something from her but she didn't push it and then said, you must be hungry so I will make something for you and your brother, yes we are starving. They sat at the table and she was cooking at the stove. She placed on the table and they looked at it and each other looks and said I am not eating this and grandma said what wrong with it? What do you mean, don't you sees those cockroaches and flies in the bowl and Owen said no you must be seeing things so if you feel that you don't want to eat don't eat it, it is an sign, I don't understand what you are saying we should have stayed with mom and dad and we were been fine, because we were born there and we have died too and I know the scenario but I am willing to live with grandma and we will have an good life and about an minute later she was not in the room and Oliver said where have she gone I don't know and they looks around and she was not there and don't eat Oliver, I am not where have she gone too?

Your asking me I was with you and she just vanished in thin air and now we are alone in this place, yes once again we are alone and we are not going anywhere at all do you understand what I am saying Oliver, Owen said well maybe we should go and Oliver said no that grandma will have the suspicious about us so we are not moving so, they sat in the kitchen and now it was getting dark and Oliver was about to put the switch on and then Owen said don't, I don't understand you said don't, well there is no electricity in this place and we went to the wrong place, I don't understand what you are saying? Well this is one of the places that we when too visit grandma but that is her old place , oh I see and she move a long time ago and who is that lady?

# "LADY IN WHITE"

Who is that lady in white? Do not know I have to explain that she is a ghost. Oh I see now what you are saying, we are just running into ghosts left and right, yes and I don't like it. Come on Oliver you are scaring me and I don't like it not at one bit, but I am just telling you what going now and we are not alone so I don't understand what you are trying to says but let go and leave this place but we have tried but it bought us back for an reason, yes I know but let go now and see if we can escape the lady in white, and I think she is has bad like the man with the red beard. I agree. Later that night Oliver and Owen snuck out of window and the lady in white just appear on the end of the road and now Owen was really frighten and scare so Oliver said don't worry we will get out of here, are you sure? Yes I am sure and don't worry about it now.

Once again Owen and Oliver walks and walks and miles and miles and reach the end of the road and no houses and just woods and Owen said what now? I don't know but we need to get to the city and be safe and it will drag us back to the house, how do you know that's I just know and be don't give in, and I don't understand what you are really saying, just follow me and we will be fine.

I don't know if we should go through the woods or just go and find the main road and headed out from here. I am confused and we are lost.

But I don't want to scare you but it is the truth and I don't think we will escape our destiny, I don't like what you are saying Oliver.

About one hour later they stood under the tree and the rain fell and then the thunder and lighting occurs and Owen said we cannot stay here and not under the tree, I know that we might get stuck and end up dead.

Don't says that Oliver and I don't want to dies and I don't neither so be quiet and so they looks around and once again they saw that Lady in white, she wants us and we need to hide or run from this place immediately, yes let move it on, fine and they walks a little bit and they both were exhaust and tried and so they sat down when the rain was coming down and so about an minute later Owen got up and looks around and said Oliver I sees the highway and we can find the crossing to the city and that is wonderful and they both started to walks and they were crossing the bridge and the " Lady in white" said stop don't go there, and they kept on walking and she came closer and closer and they ran across and didn't looks back at her and now Owen and Oliver were relief and that they were safe and but they thought that they were safe but something were waited for them on the other side and Owen said I don't like this, it just don't looks right, I know what you means so we have to stayed. Why looks the bridge is gone, no I cannot believe it, once again they were trapped unknown place and Owen and Oliver didn't know how to escape this scenario and so Oliver had an plan that they had to swim in the lakes and so Owen said we are going to drown here, no we are not, we are good swimmer. Yes we are, and about half hour later, Owen and Oliver jump in the water and then they swim and then they saw something in the water and trying to grab them. Keeps swimming and don't let them grab it will drown you and me, are you serious, listen what I am saying, it is trying to reach me, no save me, I cannot, you are so far away, where are you? I don't you see. Owen disappear and Oliver looks and looks, but he was gone and about five minutes later, Oliver saw Owen head floating and so he swim to him and try to pull, him but then he was gone, Oliver said where are you and about a minute later was gone.

About one hour later Oliver, Owen would on the bottom of water and they would looking at each others eyes and they are staring at each others, then they disappear, and no trace of Owen and Oliver...

One afternoon the sun came out and Owen and Oliver standing on the edge of the water, Owen said to Oliver so what happen, yesterday? I don't remember do you remember? No but we need to go the house, the house is calling us, go we need, to go back... are you serious? We need to listens, do you hear them? Yes I do, looks at us we are not same because we are dead. No we are not. Yes we are. I don't believe and you are lying to me, no I am not you cannot even touch me, I don't understand? Did you remember anything? Stop repeating yourself and we cannot stay or go the house but you are saying that we perish, so we are gone, because you jump into and we die. So we die last night and it your entire fault, because you don't blame me, stop it, do you hear them calling us?

Yes and they are loud and getting louder and they heard the footsteps, and few shadow, coming closer and closer, the dark shadows approach us...

We stood it came close and touch my shoulder and I felt the chill and dark shadow pull through the ground, and they ended up in the house, they we would standing around, and said welcome home...

Ellie and James said why did you comes here but we would force by the dark shadow, and we told you to go far way but now you are trapped here.

Then the whole family went together, and then they are gone.

# WELCOME HOME

The house was sold about one month ago and the family, so the new family move two teenager boy and girl, and they drove up the driveway and the gate behind close, and then they step out and all teenager ran inside and the girl found the room with the flowers wallpaper, and an old chair, Tiffany said mom and dad this will be my room, I really like it very much. Tom and Tony said we like the room next door, then the parents said okay, and the master bedroom downstairs and they said fine. That evening Eve said I will make something for dinner and Tom and Tony said what are we having dinner it will be surprise.

Tiffany is a tall and medium build and brown eyes and brown hair and then Tom with about six feet tall and short hair and blue eyes and Tony are a bit short and brown hair, and friendly. So they decided to explore and Tiffany, and Tom, Tony, but then mom said be careful we will.

About one hour later, Tony find a room and he thought they would behind him but they wouldn't, so Tony walk in and then suddenly the door close and then Tony was banged on the door and said open the door.

About five minutes later, Tony was still stuck inside the room and eerie sound and some Omni sounds and the voices, then the push and then the door wide open, Tony step out and then he was push down the stairs and Tom and Tiffany said what happen, I don't know, but he was bleeding. So we need to tell my mom and dad, went they came down and the mother said what happen? I don't know, but I told you not wander off, so I need to put something on your cut, fine, so we will be eating in few minutes. Then they all sat down at the table and the mom brought out chicken wings and rice and it looks good honey, and then the flies came in and few huge cockroaches on the table.

Tiffany started to scream and said what kind food did you make mom? It the same foods like I always made but too many bugs crawls and Eve came to the table and then threw it out, so I think that we should go out to eat.

Ed said no we are going eat this foods and Tiffany said I refuse to eat it and Eve said our children are right; we should go out to eat, fine. Then Ed said let order pizza, New York style, yes I like that's, so Ed order and about half hour it was delivery, so that Ed answer the door and pay for it.

Ed bought the pizza and place on the table, and the chairs would on the side and said who is playing this practically joke, we didn't do this.

They all sat at the table and they open the box and each took a piece and then they started to eat and then they felt someone was in the room, and Ed said well kid that your imagination, but then it was gone.

Then they finish eating you kids get ready for bed but it is too early, well tomorrow, you will start the new school, we know mom.

So they all went upstairs and parents sat in the living room and about ten minute later Ed and Eve went to the door and no one was there. About one minute later it happens again! I don't understand what going on here.

Do you know and let me know? I am not sure said Ed. I am not sure what going on here but I think we should find out. Well I am going to looks around myself said Eve to Ed and I am not I have a bad feeling about it and where is Tony and Tom and Tiffany I don't know but I will called them but I will check there rooms and so Eve when upstairs and but no trace of them, and she called out to Ed and I don't know where they are? But I will go up to the upper stairs to the attic, are sure it will be safe? Of course I will be fine. Where are Tom and Tiffany and Tony, I don't hears them and they are not around and I think they are missing, no they are here, but I don't sees them. They must be hide and seeks and I don't like that and they are acting childish and I will grounded them and then Ed said maybe they are missing and strange things did happen in this house, are you going to listen to the urban legend or too me? Well Eve, I have an bad feeling about this place but you fell in love immediately with the place and I couldn't refuse to say no too you but hope the children's are all right! Then Eve heard whisperer and said I think they are doing one practical joke on us and so then Ed said I don't think so I think that we have ghosts in our home, are you crazy? No, but you never listen to me and when I heard footsteps and thought it was that I was dreaming and I was not.

About two minute later, Tiffany and Tony and Tom came and Ed said well you don't looks good and Tiffany said we are fine, dad and Eve didn't even looks at them and just kept on cooking, but the children really looks different and Ed was like scare of them and Eve was just like under an trance and so Tom and Tony came closer to there dad and whisperer ands said we were on the other side and then Josh appear and said nice too meet you all, and Eve said who is speaking and is it Tony and they answers and said no it is Josh.

Who are you? Do you hear me? Yes I do and well I guess what I have told you, you probably won't like it....

Go on Josh, I am not afraid of ghosts, well I am a ghost and you are?

# GHOSTS AROUND US

Eve started to speak to Josh like he was alive but Eve looks at me better and I don't want too, yes you are afraid and you know what I am.

Ed said looks at his children's and said to Eve I think that we loss our children's and Eve said you are crazy and they are here, sitting at the table, but they are ghosts, stop it, stop it with the nonsense and be quiet and I don't want to burn the foods, they probably will not eat it anyways, is that true? No mom, we will eat ours foods and what is your father saying, I don't know but don't listen to him and follow us to the basement we want to shown you something, it is an surprise, well okay and Ed said don't go there, why not?

About ten minutes, Ed was still sitting at the table and waiting for his dinner but Eve didn't comes back and he looked around and then Ellie and James appear ands said you must leave this house now, who are you peoples?

We lived and died here and you must get your wife and your children's before midnight, but why tomorrow will be Friday the 13th and things will happen and I think they all ready started and you don't says so!!!

But Ed knew that he should listen to the warning and he needed to save his wife from a tragedy to happen and but he didn't know how to stop it.

But somehow before she was about to be pushed down he grab her hand and said come with me and you need to listen to what I am saying and she looks at the children's and said I want to be with them, you are... just step out and we will talked and she said no I am staying but somehow Ellie pushed her out and Ed out the house and they landed on the grass and the house lights started to flicker and then she saw her children's looking out the window and she said we need to save them, but it is too late. No I want my babies back and then Rose came out the house and said it is too late you lost them to the house.

Ellie open the door and then said goodbye and the doors shut tight and Eve saw here children's in the windows of the house and Ed said now it is time for us to leave and so you are right but I need to get something in the house, no I am not going to let you go back inside, do you hear what I am saying, yes but about children's? Well, the house took them and now we need to go on living and so let go and forget about this place that I bought for you...

Eve started to argument with Ed and was angry and push him down to the ground and when toward the door and he somehow caught her and she was not in the house and then pick her up and took her into the car and close the door and then started up the engine and left in the hurried and Eve was sad and furious with Ed but he didn't care. We are leaving this place now and we are not coming back do you hear what I am saying? :Loud and clear and let go now, so they drove off from the long driveway and headed off to the road and headed toward 287 route and so they just kept on driving and so they didn't stop and talked about what happen and meanwhile back at the house, the children were playing and so it was loud and Josh didn't like it at all and then said to be quiet and then it got suddenly dark and the doors shut tight and it was time for them to go to sleep and about an hour later, the wind blow in and then it just got peaceful and quiet and then the rain came and it fell hard.

The next day came and Eve and Ed were far away from the house and felt like pressure was release and Ed said don't you feel better about leaving and some matter that Eve was a bit, you know something we are not alone, how do you know I just feel it and so I think that we were follow and I think it want us to come back to the house and don't listen to the voices they are trying to trick us. I am not listening and so we will fight it and we will be fine. Are you sure about it? Yes I am, sure we will be safe, and how do you know? I don't know. Not sure about it then the voices and the eerie sound...

The footsteps would get louder and louder and voices would loud and Ed and Eve, I don't want to stay here. So we leave where here and they will follow us, maybe they won't! I am not going take the chance and I am staying and trying to beat them, you don't even sees them and you are going to beat them come on Ed who are you kidding.. We are beaten by the ghosts.

This one has the red hair and red beard and he looks evil and he is coming closer to us and I don't like it at all and so we need to know how to get rid of the ghosts that follows us from that house and so we need to find an plan and make the ghost go into the light, that will not be easy to do but I am willing to tried it, Ed I know that you can do it and I will be fine.

I don't even see the ghosts I sees the dark shadow in front of you. You do so why don't help me to tell it go into the light.

Don't let it touch you, you might dies and I don't want it to happen and I don't understand your gibbering? I am not gibbering I am trying to explains that seem like we never left the house, now your not making sense.

We drove off into the road and left the area and now your saying that we are still in the house, looks around Ed and tell me what you see? Some old pictures that were in the house and why are they here, the previously

# ARE WE DEAD NOW!

Do you hear that sound? It is coming from the basement and it sound like it coming up toward us, so let move away and tried to open the door and get out of here, did you sees that' s? What was it? I don't know but I am not staying when we move it move and it staring at us right now and so just stand and let it touch us or we move from it? I say we move right now and we just get the heck out of here and I don't where to go! Then the lights flicker and then the doors shut tight and now we are stuck here and nowhere to run.

It is following us and it want us to be here has an resident, no ways and they saw Tiffany and Tom and Tony coming closer and closer and they didn't look friendly but evil, they are not ours children they are trying to trick us.

I will tried to open the door and you run for your life, got it and so will you, yes I will you promised, of course and I do not want to be stuck in this house and this place so I just to be with you.. Good and let do it now... but this house somehow manage to bring us back into the house, I know maybe because the children were born there and they died there too.

But the sound and the walls would creaking and creaking and the bloods was flowing on the walls and floors and and it was breaking glasses and lifting up the kitchen table and chairs and then it just stop it now.

About an minute later, it began to happen again and again and somehow they crawl on the floor and someone pick up ED and threw him against the wall and then Eve when close to him and he was breathing very swallow and she said what have done to my husband? But nothing so then it came close to Eve and pick her up to the ceiling and drop her and she hit her head and she was near Ed and she was bleeding from the head and about five minutes later they took there last breathe and she looks at him and smile and kiss him and then she somehow was looking at her body above her and said no, no why did it happen to me? Then he children and husband surrounded her and said we are home and the Omni sound was silent for the night and Eve looks around and said we are home now. Yes we are darling, and she kisses him and walks away into the walls. He was gone and Eve then follow him and they were not there anymore and Tiffany and Tony and Tom and the whole family were together again and so that they didn't roam the house and then Josh said somehow they mange to leave and so they just left how could they? I don't know but I just saw them leaving and they were able too, so they are not bound to this place like we are.

I don't understand they got killed in the perimeter and how come they could escape these, and Eve and Ed and the family walks out to the yard and they were relief that they were not control by the man with the red beard and red hair and so they walks and walks but somehow never left the yard.

Whatever happen still didn't leave the yard and saw tombstones that were over 100 year old and said Eve said I don't like it here and we are stuck here, maybe we can just go and the children's said no we cannot leave we are going back into the house, no I don't allow you to do so.. He is calling my name and I said no you are staying here. About one hour later, Ed said let the children's go and no I will not let back into that house and they should stayed with us.

No, go Tom, Tony, Tiffany, they just walks in the door shut close and then Eve said I didn't want them going back and you allow them and I am mad at you and you will not sleep with me, so I am in the dog house. Yes because you when behind me and gave the children's permission to go into that house.

Honey accept it and we will be going back soon and we will not roam the yard and the streets, I am not going back inside and so if you will be alone outside here, Eve, I rather be alone then hang out with those shadow peoples. Fine, be stubborn and so be alone. Okay!

Ed walks inside and looks around and knows one was there and he just kept on walking and ran into James and Ellie and said where Eve is? Still outside and then the thunder and lighting occurs and Eve ran inside and hold Ed very tight and they said the man with the red beard is very angry at you both leaving.

Let him be mad and I don't be here, but you became a resident when you bought the house, fine, said Eve to James…

The rain came pouring down and the lighting stuck the house and a bit of smoke and it seem like it was a fire…

Later that night the walls were bleeding and the steps and the house shook and the doors and windows were closing and opening and then the door hinge pull off and the door was on the ground and then a lot of whisperer and footsteps were coming closer it was the dark shadow coming closer to Ellie and James and Eve and Ed and he touch James and he flew off the ground and into the floor and Ellie was screaming and James said don't worry I am fine and some blood griping from his face and hands and then he said Ellie don't be scare I will be near you soon… will you?

Later when the mist and the smoke was gone and the red hair man was gone and now they were relief for an while and then it was an boom and then it was more dark shadow and not only the red hair beard man coming it was more than him, and they knew the evil, but James and Ellie and Ed and Eve were very frighten, of him and you know that we are trapped in this house, yes I know because this house draw us here and now we live in this house and we have no choice when we got killed here and now we are trapped and then Rose appear and said stop whiny and you are giving me an headache, and they kept to themselves and then Josh said I have an idea to escape when new owner move in we will scare them out of the house and we will follow, and maybe they will follow us, I hope not... do you think so, probably. No, they will not coming do you see them? Yes, they are behind us, will they catch us and then what?

Tried to bring us to the house and turns us into "GHOSTS" no I will not be dead and I want to be alive, so do I? So let somehow lose them, but how can you lose ghosts, I don't know... Eve called out too Ed and so wait for me...

I am but don't be so slow and I am trying to catch up too you and I think we will somehow to get out of the woods and lose the " ghosts" and I think they are like shadow following us and so they wants us to be resident at the house.

But I will not said Eve and Ed agree and then Ellie and James said don't looks at us and so just go way from the house and far, far way and you do get what I am saying. They ran and ran into circle and ended back at the house at the front door and almost inside and but somehow didn't get inside and then fell to the ground and then got up and ran out of the yard. Suddenly appear Rose and Josh and the other ghosts, and standing at the end of the yard and not letting them leave, but Ellie somehow push one of them out the way and got through.

It not going to works they wants them both and they will get them don't you get? I thought they were far way and now they are inside and trapped like we are and there is no escape do you hear what I am saying they got possession to enter and now they will be like us, I need to tried to get them out now.. Too late, what should we do now?

No it is not too late, listens Owen and Oliver you must leave now and you will be safe and they both said no we are staying we have no place to go.

Yes you do just leave I am begging you to go now, no! Don't

be stubborn right now just go and we will be fine, your not fine but you are dead and I can sees you and dad so are staying, you know that you and your brother will end up dead too? Yes that why we came back because we are a family and we should stick together no matter what?

# POSSESSION BY THE HOUSE

Owen and Oliver felt an draft and then an chill on there shoulder and then Josh appear, and said you two stupid boys are trapped in this house and you had the chance and you blow it and how could you, I never had the chance but you too did and why didn't just left the house, well the house told us to stayed and we did, you know that went it happened you will be dead.

Yes but this must be our destiny to be in this house, no, no you were trick like two little boys that your parents wanted you but the man with the red beard trick you and now you will be resident of this wonderful house, that ghosts live but they don't leave...

I can deal that's and are sure your parents are really here? Yes they are and I am glad to be backing home where I belonged, well well for you.

The dark shadows coming out of the wall, trying to grab the living and Owen and Oliver said we are ghosts, and we need to scare them away now. But what do we need chase them away, so you make, them run, wait a minute they are not alive what do you mean? They are dead like we are. No! Yes they are. Stop!

I don't understand but they are just like us and so stop chasing them, okay now you think it fun and it and game but this is the place where we live forever and that doesn't change at all.

That true what you are saying but I don't like the dark shadow lurking at us and we are stuck here, I know that's and so I know it is real, so let find mom and dad and so we can be an family again.

Kathy and Katie step in and said it dark and pitch black here and I have an bad feeling about this place, you do, and then the door slammed shut tight and Katie said did you sees those globes, I don't understand what you are saying didn't anything touch you? I thought it was you, no, I didn't do it.

Kathy said let try open the door and gets the hell out of this house, and then the door was open. Now I am scare of my life and we are stuck inside of this house, I don't like the practical joke that you are playing, I am not Katie.

This shit is shit is happening for real, I don't believe just an moment ago I saw an dark shadow lurking at me, it was an ugly face. Katie when ahead of Kathy and hid in the corner and Katie came by and Kathy jump out, and Katie was very angry and so what do we do? How do we escape that demons that wants to possession us I don't know but we better hurried and figure out how to get out of the house and I do not want to died here, do you hear what I am saying that was an bad idea coming to this house, I know but now we need to run and open that door and Kathy said well I don't see the door in front of me and we lost our flashlight and it is pitch black here, and Katie said did you touch me? No someone did and I don't like it here, and it is really cold here and I see the cold and chill in the air, and then it was an eerie sound approach them and Katie said it wants us and I don't know how we will find the ways out. We are trapped and I think that we are dead, no we are not that entity is trying to trick us and you don't looks at it now, do you understand and we are stronger and we will be the odd of being stuck in this house forever, how do you know that we are struck all ready and I don't like being here, I hears you loud and clear, so let find the ways out. The entity were not move Kathy and Katie were very scare and didn't know what was happening too them. I cannot move and it is holding us here and we shouldn't have gone inside and I don't know if we will ever get out, you are scaring me but it is the truth, I cannot take it...

Listen carefully somehow quietly we sneak out and we run for our lives...

But don't look back and just run and don't worry about me, your my friend and I bought you here but I came here on my free will.

Yes you did and I am sorry that I came here and the man with the red hair is staring at us and don't look into his eyes, I won't.

About a minute later, Katie looks at Kathy and said now we run to the door and run, and run, then a chill came over and eerie sound and Omni sound and footsteps were near them. They saw there own breathe of cold...

# TRAPPED FOREVER

Kathy and Katie were trying to escape and get out of the house and Katie and went you get near the door, make sure that you open the door and run for your life. about you., I will be in back of you, I promise. So Katie saw the opportunity of getting out and she ran to the door and when outside and she looks around and Kathy was not there and she wanted to go back., and then the door close shut and Katie knew that she had leaves that place but she wanted to get her friend free from that haunted house. Katie just stood and stare at the house and she was about to go back inside but then she saw Kathy near her and she was relieve and so they both walk toward the road and headed out of the yard, but Katie notice that Kathy was not herself.

They walk a mile down the road and Kathy said, I cannot leave. Katie said why not I think that I am all ready "dead" you don't looks like it.

The closer that she got to the road, it were not let her go, and she said to Katie, you must leave and I need to go back into the house, what are saying?

I am saying sorry friend, and it happen to me and we will be always friends. No you are coming with me, do hear me? Yes but it will not let me go...

Fight it and be strong and comes with me... I cannot move and it is pulling me back to the house and you need to go alone home and you will be safe. I will miss you and I really need you and can you come with me. No I cannot you go alone and promise that you will never come back to this house.

I cannot promise you that I want to be with you, you don't want to be here.

You don't want to be trapped in the house of ghosts; you want to be among the living. That was the last day that she saw Kathy and she walks away and Katie just walks for miles and miles until she reach the highway. She didn't look back and never been seen again… Kathy and Katie were friends forever. Katie was never went to the house and never when out of her home. Katie was afraid of her life because of the haunting, that she when through, and Katie was not sure if it was real, or all in her mind. But Katie just keep to herself and doesn't leave her home anymore but seem to bought something back with her and watcher her and she has the fears in her eyes, that she is in danger.

But Katie looks around and she says " I am not home" I am trapped in the haunted house and she screams and she vanished in thin air.